TRUCKER JOE

JORGI

This story was inspired by Nádine.

CONTENTS

With great thanks to my entire family for their ever loving support. And once again a special thank you to my sister for all her hard work.

CHAPTER ONE

It was very dark that night. He felt that he couldn't see properly, hence the slow speed. Joe suddenly slammed on the brakes. He thought he saw a white shape in the road. He wasn't quite sure, but came to a screeching halt anyway. He looked more closely; his daunting green eyes searched every corner of the two narrow beams. The truck's beams helped, but not greatly. So he decided to step out of his 'homey' cab.

He gently, quietly lowered his tall frame to the ground, hanging on to the guard rail as he did so. He knew his truck very well, thus he knew where to look and how to look.

He stepped slowly around the front end making his way to the back, cautiously. He heard a sound, faint at first. He couldn't be sure what he heard. So he listened more closely. There it was again!

He turned around, realising that it came from the front two tyres. He looked and listened more carefully. Then he saw a white, hairy thing sticking out from behind the black rubber.

"Oh my God!" he exclaimed when he saw the whole white shape for the very first time. He bent down to seem less scary and gently picked up the little shape to get a better look.

It was a tiny, tiny dirty-white pup. It had a black spot on its little back and a brown-and-black patch on its side. When he saw the little guy's (oh yeah, it's a boy) face Joe smiled. His tiny face looked like it was masked in a lively brown colour. He smiled again – what a cute, little fella.

He returned to his cab and gently placed the little one, that couldn't have been more than four months old, on the fabric seat next to him. He needed time to think. He needed to weigh his options.

A sudden yelp brought him back to his new companion. The pup started moving about on the soft seat in a very clumsy manner. That yelp, that little yelp, just confirmed what he should do, what he needed to do, what he wanted to do: go home. Right now, before he changed his mind again.

Home. It sounded so good to Joe. Home. He thought of *his* home with mixed feelings. And about going home, even more so. He couldn't remember the last time he had been there. Was it good? Was it bad? It all seemed and felt blurry to him. No wonder, he thought, being drunk half the time, perhaps even, most of the time, would cause such blurry, faded memories. Was he mad for wanting to go back? For wanting to see what he had left behind? And who he had left behind? Would *she* even remember him? Joe?

All these harrowing questions made him reconsider. "Do I really want to go home?" he asked aloud, hoping that it would give him some clarity. He felt scared, really scared. Imagine a man his size feeling this way – scared. He didn't know what to expect. Lucky for him, it was a *long* way home!

So it would seem that Joe, trucker Joe, was going home. At long last he was going home...

Pup's whimpering gave him temporary relief from his haunting thoughts, and his haunting memories. He looked at Pup (for lack of a better, more suitable name) who lay all bundled up on the large seat next to him.

He must be hungry, Joe thought, and estimated the nearest truck stop. Five miles, hmm, it's not that far. "I suppose you'll make it, won't you?" he asked little Pup and gave him a quick pat on his tiny white back. Joe was still taken aback by his small size; how could anyone chuck away such a cute, little fella?

He shook his head in disbelief and told Pup that he, Joe, would never abandon him. Never.

This was quite a change for Joe, considering his messy past. And this was just a dog!

He shook his curly head, again in disbelief. Who was this man, he asked himself perplexed. The Joe Mountain he knew would never have taken in a dog, let alone, a young one. Joe was a loner, who never really cared for others. He let people do their own thing and let them go their own way. He felt that this worked for him; way better than to be held up by others and their emotional needs. Always those emotional needs, he thought frustrated.

He was never really good at tending to those needs, hence, the bottle. The sweet, comforting taste of the bottle. Probably his best companion. At least up until a few years ago; it was then that he had a serious crash. A serious meltdown.

He never touched the bottle ever again, not even a single drop. Joe Mountain had gone completely dry. He had his fill, and that was enough for him. It was time to move on, even if it meant doing it alone. He was used to that, actually, for in his head he always stood alone...

Again, he slammed on the brakes; he almost missed the turn to the brightly lit truck stop.

CHAPTER TWO

The brightly lit truck stop was crawling with people and cars and trucks (his favourite). It was the only place where he felt that he could be himself, just Joe. Nothing more, nothing less. Just Joe.

He found the perfect spot for his long hauler. This wasn't just any hauler; it was his favourite, and more than that: it was his. Joe's truck. Everybody knew that, and they respected it.

Joe crossed the busy parking lot with Pup safely tucked away in his oversized jacket. He didn't care whether it was allowed or not, or even proper for that matter. He was taking Pup with, and that was that. Besides, they were both in need of food, good food. The more, the better! He smiled and patted his relaxed mid-section; Joe was completely aware of his big belly, but it didn't bother him, not in the least.

He finally entered the crowded diner, and was lucky enough to procure the very last open booth for him and Pup. On his way he passed many interesting faces. These faces were each so different and so unique in their own way. He studied a few of them while he waited for one of the two waitresses. This suited Joe best – him and Pup in their own corner and the rest of the world in the other. He preferred people at a distance; he did not like it when they got too close, not one bit!

"What'll ye have?" one of the two waitresses asked in a very lazy manner. Joe could barely make out her mumbling question. He looked closely at her. She didn't seem very friendly as she impatiently tapped her notebook with her chewed pencil.

Joe politely looked at her and then at his sticky menu. Her frown deepened and her tapping got louder. Joe ignored her apparent impatience and continued looking over his menu with intense focus. His light framed glasses rested patiently on the tip of his gnome-like nose. He finally spoke.

"I would like a coffee. Cream, no sugar. And then a toasted sandwich. Cheddar cheese and tomato with extra onions. Fried onions, please. And also an extra large portion of fries. Thank you," he ended his very specific order. He had to have enough for both of them.

"Is that all?" she lazily asked and gave him a very bored, vacant look.

"That's all, thank you."

She turned without a word, and lazily shuffled along the worn-out aisle. Strange bird, he thought as he checked on Pup. Pup was sleeping at the moment, but he knew that the instant their food arrived, Pup would be wide awake, sniffing the air with his over-active, tiny nose. Trying very hard to draw the delicious food to him via his incessant sniffing.

Joe smiled nostalgically at the image his mind

conjured up for him. Aye, all these memories, a lifetime's worth, and all he could remember was bits and pieces. Only a few, clear images. The rest still remained blurry, faded from his consciousness, faded from his life... How sad, he thought, almost letting a tear loose.

"Here you go," the lazy waitress announced and almost dropped the plates loudly on his angular table. Joe felt relieved that the sudden wetness decided to hesitate. He was in a public place after all, in a room filled with strangers. And there was one standing right by his side, a very unfriendly one at that.

"Thanks," he replied softly, still shook-up by his sudden nostalgia.

"Ur coffee's coming." Again shuffling away with her prominent posterior shuffling in tune. Hopefully his coffee would get to him while it's hot, and before he finished his meal.

Joe checked unobtrusively to see if anyone was watching. No one was. Everyone seemed to be either lost in their busy-busy conversations or completely involved in their eating. He was safe, Pup was safe, and it was safe to sneak pieces of food to the little fella – who was wide awake just as he predicted.

Joe smirked and gave half a snort as he prepared to give Pup his first bite. He thought it a good idea to start with the fries. They were fatty and it would fill his belly fairly quickly.

"What are you doing?" Joe almost dropped the small piece of potato, shaken by the unexpected vocal presence. He looked up, trying very hard to keep his cool. He immediately relaxed. It was not either of the two waitresses asking the question. It was in fact a blue-haired female teenager looking right at him.

"What are you doing?" she asked again, a bit rudely according to Joe.

"'cuse me," Joe's lazy waitress came to his rescue. This time, she gently placed his cup of steaming coffee in front of him. The frothy cream she placed next to his white cup and saucer, also gently. His surprised look, he could not hide.

"You're welcome," the waitress said sweetly with a slight smile, showing off dimples he didn't know she had. He wondered briefly whether she knew she had them – two, deep dimples. Who would have guessed?

'Blue-girl', that was how Joe nicknamed the young teenager, just stood there looking wide eyed at the both of them. As soon as his friendly waitress had left, 'Blue-girl' uninvitedly made herself comfortable at his booth.

Joe wasn't quite sure what to do. He wanted so dearly to be alone and get rid of her, rather quickly, *and* he still had to feed poor Pup – the wee fella was probably very hungry by now. Damn this girl. How will he rid them of her?

He gave her the sternest most disgruntled look he could muster. Maybe if he did that long enough and well enough, he would be able to scare her off. After all, she was just a 'little' girl, right? Even with her glowing bright blue hair.

"What are you doing, Mister?" she asked amidst his very unhappy thoughts.

"I can see the small bump beneath your jacket," she said rather challenging.

Joe was left speechless for a minute or two by this forward teen who was quite mouthy for her age.

Again, he gave her a disgruntled look, but coloured with more irritation. He even narrowed his dark green eyes and frowned deeply to stress his pressing impatience for her to leave and his irritation which was beginning to turn into mild frustration. His food was getting cold, not even mentioning his coffee!

If there was one thing Joe did not like, it would probably be cold coffee, and his was nearing that point...

All of a sudden 'Blue-girl' stood up. She gave him one last look, an intense one; her blue eyes almost shone as brightly as her noticeable blue hair.

"See you, Mister," she said abruptly and looked like someone had deflated her balloon.

She left, with her shoulders slouching a bit. Joe felt a tad bit sorry for her and slightly guilty for being so anti-social. He knew full well that he can be a bit of a Neanderthal at times, but he was this way for a very good reason.

A soft yelp coming from his brown jacket made him soon forget about 'Blue-girl' and about his uncomfortable feelings.

CHAPTER THREE

It was a lone Joe Mountain who walked slowly towards his lone truck, or so he thought. In fact, he was not alone, not by a long shot. Inside his oversized brown jacket, there was a warm, curled up bundle of white fur. Behind his silent truck was a young girl with shiny, blue hair...

Joe got inside his familiar, blue-and-silver truck. The truck stop had quiet down a bit and Joe felt that he could relax; being *inside* his truck also helped. It always felt like home to him, even if it was a very small home. Home, it was.

With Pup resting peacefully next to him, Joe pressed the red button and his silent truck roared into life. He sat there for a minute or two just appreciating the pleasing sound coming from the massive front. He slipped the gear lever in first and got ready to hit the road again. But something caught his eye, something blue it would seem. He turned his curly head all the way back to get a better look – it was 'Blue-girl', none other than cheeky mouthy 'Blue-girl'.

Joe felt a pull, an uneasy pull in the pit of his full stomach. He knew this particular feeling all too well. And it wasn't a pleasant one. So he braced himself for what was coming.

"Hey, Mister." 'Blue-girl' was already standing by his elevated, open window. Did his window really have to be open? He asked himself, almost reproachfully. Joe took a minute or two, weighing his limited options, before he looked at her. He knew that his previous look would not help this time; 'Blue-girl' knew it and the parking lot lighting wasn't working to his advantage.

"Hey Mister, can you hear me?" she asked so innocently in her forward manner. He probably took too long to react. What exactly was he supposed to say to this blue-haired teen who happened to be a human? He tried his best to avoid them, that is, people.

Joe dared winding down his window fully; he did not want to attract any unwanted attention. He had no choice, he would have to engage this forward, yet peculiar teen – she had left him no other option with her nagging behaviour.

Joe rested his elbow on the windowless frame and looked down at her, pretending to be in a real hurry. He even revved the engine a bit to support his case.

"Very cute," he heard her say in her usual sassy manner. She even had a matching facial expression. Joe could not help but smile at this inexperienced blue-haired teen. These youngsters think they know everything, but they don't. At their tender age, they hardly know anything. What exactly do they know about life, about love, about hardship?

"Can I help you?" Joe, at long last, uttered his very first words in 'Blue-girl's presence. 'Blue-girl' just sneered at him; it was now her turn to be rude. In any case, that was how she perceived this enormously big cave-man. 'Cave-man'. Hmm, what a good name for this awkward truck-driver. She decided to christen him 'Cave-man' then and there. Now *she* was the one smiling, flashing her snow-white teeth.

Joe took notice. He wasn't good at this game, the 'getting-on-with-people' game, but for some reason he was willing to give it a go.

"Can I help you?" he asked again, a little friendlier this time. 'Blue-girl' looked at him warily, suspiciously. What brought on this sudden change in 'Cave-man', she asked herself. All of a sudden she didn't feel so sure of herself. With her forwardness in her back pocket for now, she asked 'Cave-man' carefully: "Where are you headed?" She watched him carefully as she waited for his reply.

Joe felt better at what he saw. 'Blue-girl' seemed less intimidating and it suddenly felt easier for him to respond.

"I'm headed north, towards Deckerville. Why? Do you need a lift?"

"It doesn't matter where I'm going, so long as it's out of here," 'Blue-girl' answered showing some trust. "Just away from here," she added, hoping that it would convince 'Cave-man' to give her a ride. She desperately wanted to get away, as far away as possible. She needed to do that now, right now. Every second counts.

"Hop in," Joe instinctively invited 'Blue-girl' to get in, "but before you do," he stopped her enthusiasm with an outstretched arm, the palm of his big hand, facing her. "I need to know a few things." He stopped abruptly, letting his words sound very ominous.

'Blue-girl' stopped dead in her tracks. What now, she wondered. Is he reconsidering? Is he getting cold feet? She sure as hell, hoped not!

Joe looked at her curiously and then dared his first question. "How old are you?"

At first, 'Blue-girl' wanted to be offended by his intrusive question, but then she had second thoughts. She reminded herself, hastily, that she desperately needed this ride (out of town!).

"How old am I? What business is that of yours?" You're only offering me a ride, that part she had left out for the sake of speeding up the smooth course of their parley. She really did not feel like quarrelling. All she wanted, was to get out of here, the sooner, the better. And also, it was rather late and she felt tired from all her emotional turbulence. She really hoped that...

"So, how old are you, really?" Joe pushed again for knowing her age. He had a thing for doing the right thing, and right now, that was to know her age – he did not want any trouble. He had enough of that to last him a lifetime!

"Seventeen," she answered convincingly with a straight face and then, all of a sudden, she burst out laughing after she saw his shocked face. 'Blue-girl' threw her ID at him and stood there awaiting his next silly question. She even tapped her foot to emphasize her discontentment.

This bothered Joe a bit, but he took a look at her identification card nonetheless. He had to be sure. Satisfied that she was legal, he passed her ID back. Silly or not, he had two more questions, and if 'Blue-girl' wanted that lift, she had better answer them, truthfully.

"Are you running from something or someone? Like the LAW perhaps?" he asked without batting an eyelid. As he mentioned earlier, he had a thing for doing the right thing. Giving her a ride necessarily involved him, his life *and* his truck, his beloved Nancy.

Nancy was all he had at this moment, except for his newest companion, Pup. But he was just a dog, not to be disrespectful or disparaging. Being around humans was different, very different and sometimes impossible. So, in a way, he was super glad for having Pup around – it sure made things light again.

"The Law? Are you being serious right now? The Law!" 'Blue-girl' again showed her forwardness, her cheekiness. But this time, it did not bother Joe one bit; he knew that he was winning this one, even though he wasn't the best player. He must admit, he was rather a bit rusty, okay, okay, maybe a lot.

"No, I'm not running from the Law. I'm not running from anything. I'm not running, period!" 'Blue-girl' said harshly, adamantly. She was getting annoyed by his stupid questions, and it was getting harder to contain her irritation. He was just wasting time, my time, she thought angrily.

Maybe, this was a bad idea. Maybe, she should make a duck while she still could...

"Can you hold your liquor?" Joe asked, bringing her thought-train to a complete standstill. She was totally speechless; 'Blue-girl' was speechless, she didn't know what to say!

Joe started shaking, his whole body shook with rumbling laughter. It bellowed out of his colossal mass, out of his truck into 'Blue-girl's face, into her ears. His green eyes started watering so intense was his burst of laughter.

'Blue-girl' stood there, dimly lit, next to Nancy in complete silence. She wasn't sure what to make of this man, this cave-man. He was extremely hard to read and it made communicating with him, very difficult. Should she be mad or should she join him in his mad laughter?

"Seriously though, do you drink? Do you take drugs? I have a right to know, you know," he said it defensively. It was his truck after all. Joe didn't want any trouble, therefore no druggies, and she should know this beforehand.

'Blue-girl' smiled. This one was easy. She pulled up her black sleeves and proudly displayed her clean arms. This was one thing she could resist and felt extremely proud of it. It's a miracle these days, avoiding drugs, her mom always said. That's why she was even more proud of her accomplishment – it meant that she somehow managed to spite her own mother! It also gave her a secret kick, because everyone assumed that she was some sort of druggy, some sort of lost cause. All that, from her bright, shoulder-length, blue hair!

Just when she thought that 'Cave-man' was now smiling because he was satisfied, he asked another question!

"How well do you get on with pets, dogs?" he asked, this time he gave her a steady, earnest stare. This creeped her out a bit, but not for long. Because the very next moment, Joe held a small, white bundle in his sizeable hands, "We won't be travelling alone."

CHAPTER FOUR

After about an hour's drive, 'Blue-girl' decided to break the ice a little. "What is your name?" she asked whilst playing with Pup's tiny ears. I can't keep calling you 'Cave-man', she silently thought as she looked down at the sleeping form on her lap.

"You can call me, Joe. Just Joe. That'll be fine," he tried compensating for his lack in social skills – he might be missing a few, or maybe even more.

Joe, that's a mighty name for a mighty man, she thought. She wasn't absolutely sure, but she already saw glimpses of that man. He wasn't really a 'Cave-man'; he just pretended to be one, same as her, pretending, that's all it was. Her pretence was in fact a defence mechanism, only meant to cover up her soft side, her vulnerable side. The side she thought that people might abuse or perhaps misuse if she wasn't careful, guarded.

Her 'wildling' appearance did just that – provide cover, protection. Her favourite black outfit also didn't hurt; it portrayed her 'wildling' persona, beautifully!

"What's your name?" 'Blue-girl' hadn't even noticed that Joe was repeating her question and she was supposed to answer. "What?" she asked, masking her wandering mind and making up time. If there was a subject she avoided at all cost it would be talking about herself. 'Blue-girl' did not like talking about herself and had hoped that the electric blue hair and the grim black clothing, would either scare people off, or at the very least throw them off!

But strangely enough, 'Cave-man', Joe, was immune to all that. How was that even possible, she asked herself while shaking her head. Looking at this man, who was so obviously hermitic, you would think that he would still be running after just one encounter with her, 'Blue-girl', 'Freaky-girl'.

"Look, I'm tired. It was a long day and I see that you have a bunk back there. Would you mind if I..." 'Blue-girl' didn't even get to finish her sentence. Joe was very eager to please her, for some weird reason. She thought that he wanted to be alone, safe in his own world. Joe knew the real reason. And he wasn't sharing, not yet anyway.

'Blue-girl' didn't need any encouragement. Before you could say knife, she was back there, getting ready to sleep. Partially escaping more questions, but mostly she was dog-tired.

Joe enjoyed the few hours of alone-time. He was thankful for that; he knew that it wouldn't be like this for long. Soon she would wake and then... then he would have to relate with the world again, incidentally through this girl, 'Blue-girl'. He should really try and get her name, she deserved something better than

'Blue-girl'.

Joe was playing around with the stations when he heard a sound coming from his sleeping cab. It sounded like 'Blue-girl' was returning to the living. He could hear her yawning, lazy yawns. She probably stretched out a little, not that there was a whole lot of room for that. Then finally her blue head popped around the seventies-yellow coloured curtain.

"Hello there," she greeted spiritedly. She seemed to be in a very good mood. This pleased Joe and it also gave him courage for his unavoidable contact with 'Blue-girl' (still don't know her name, he thought silently).

"Mornin'," Joe greeted back, but not so spiritedly. Whenever people were near, especially this close, he always inched back into his familiar and safe shell. That was where Joe chose to live and operate from, from within his Joe-shell. *His* shell.

"What are we going to do today?" 'Blue-girl' asked as if she was a part of this haul. This amused Joe a tiny bit. It would seem that this girl had many layers, blue layers, and it would take quite some time, to peel them all back. Maybe then he'd be able to see what she was really about. But in the end, God would only know what he would find.

"We're nearing the next town and I thought it a good idea to stretch out there and get a bite to eat. I suppose you and Pup are starving."

"Why do you call him Pup?" she asked not accusingly, although it felt that way to Joe. Was she accusing him of giving Pup a poor name?

"What I mean is, he is so cute, he deserves a proper name. One with more character. What about Casey?" Before Joe could even make a sound, she just steamrolled ahead, "My brother's name was Casey. Why don't *we* name him Casey? It is a he, isn't it?" She carried on like she was on something. Joe was completely speechless; he wasn't used to this much talking, let alone the speed with which she could converse. Wow!

"I think it, a good name for Pup. Casey," she continued without taking a breath, "I like it. I like it a lot!"

"I suppose it's a good name," Joe finally got a word in, "but I would miss Pup..."

"Pup, oops, Casey is still here, he's not gone, you know!" again showing her forwardness. She was almost being impudent, Joe thought to himself. He actually liked it, to his surprise, he liked her cheeky nature. It somehow reminded him of his daughter. His daughter. Ahh.

"There it is, there it is," she almost jumped in her seat as she pointed towards the giant peach. Poor Pup, ogh Casey, nearly fell off her lap, but she had him, safely in her delicate hands. He joined in the excitement with his little yelps; he could not bark yet, at least not properly. Joe leaned over and gave him a quick pat on his tiny, white head. 'Blue-girl' laughed and also cuddled his hairy ears. His hair was so soft to the touch, it was remarkable, 'Blue-girl' noticed quietly.

She was a bit nervous, not quite sure why, but she could feel a tense tingling sensation taking hold of her young shoulders. That was a sure tell tale sign, she was nervous, but why, she wondered, feeling unsettled all of a sudden.

"If you had a camera, you could have taken the most spectacular pictures. This area is well-known for its breathtaking scenery. You'll see what I mean, in just a bit," Joe tried hard being less of a cave-man and more sociable, more human it would seem.

'Blue-girl' took the bait. In a flash she had her thin cell phone out and was taking pictures like it was going out of style. This also pleased Joe, because sharing these beautiful surroundings was extremely satisfying to him. Was he beginning to change, he asked himself lacing his question with a bit of panic.

After a few more minutes and a few more miles, Joe found what he was looking for. His next stop wasn't actually a truck stop. It was in fact a small diner which happened to be encased by vast, open space. This open space was coincidentally big enough for trucks, for his Nancy. It made manoeuvring about in his massive 18-wheeler, a breeze. Cathy's diner was also adventitiously located close to major highways.

Joe safely parked his Big Rig closest to the familiar diner. Familiar not in the sense that he knew everybody, except for dear old Cathy, but familiar in the sense that *this* diner felt like a second home. It was quiet, not that busy, therefore Joe felt as though he could disappear into one of their cosy corners. The family-owned diner also let Joe go about his business, his way. Obviously, this also held great appeal for Joe, especially now with little Casey and his newest travelling companion, 'Blue-girl', by his side.

CHAPTER FIVE

They sat quietly, Joe and 'Blue-girl' and the wee fella, looking over their menus. Although Joe knew this menu by heart, he still looked at it with intense focus. Being around people, especially this close, was still new to him, and also, being out of his comforting truck always left him feeling 'naked', AND he wasn't fond of that feeling! Hiding behind his large menu, somehow helped.

"So, what's your name?" he asked casually, hoping that this time, he would get an answer – he was getting tired of using his nick-name for her. She deserved better than just 'Blue-girl'.

She looked at him funny, buying some time as usual. Her blue hair looked more wavy than yesterday. Maybe it was his rather flat pillow. Joe didn't like these modern, puffed-up pillows. He believed that it was bad for your neck, and these days, his body needed all the help he could give it.

"Why are you so keen on knowing my name?" she asked matter-of-factly; her usual forwardness, forgotten for the moment. Joe was thrown for an instant, and felt greatly relieved when Cathy, with her big smile, came to take their order.

"What will it be today?" she asked while looking at both of them. Cathy didn't mind dogs, especially one as cute as Casey. In any case, she has known Joe for quite some time. He might display himself strangely and awkwardly to the world, but Cathy knew that under all that unnecessary veneer, was a good, decent man.

"I'll have my usual, thank you Cathy. Oh, and something extra for little Pup over there." Pup was resting quietly on 'Blue-girl's lap, only his little ears showed signs of life.

Cathy nodded and gave a quick wink as she wrote down Joe's usual order. Then she turned towards the unusual teen with the striking, blue hair. Cathy didn't know what to make of this one. But she kept her cool, and waited patiently for the girl to open her thin mouth.

"I'll just have a salad," she surprised them both as she finally answered, absent-mindedly. It was almost as though she tried to be invisible, not making any eye-contact. Was she trying to hide, Cathy wondered and left with her usual, "Okey-doke. I'll be right back."

"Blue Bell," 'Blue-girl' blurted out of the blue. Joe was almost startled by her sudden words. He removed his reading-glasses and looked at her, at her delicate face with the wild bluish hair and didn't say a word. He didn't want to scare her off.

"My name is Blue Bell," she said it slowly this time, emphasizing every word. Now she gave him a full-on stare, her forwardness was back in all its glory.

Joe – cursed or blessed, depending on which way

you looked at it – with his limited people-skills didn't know what to say. What do you say to that, anyway? 'Blue Bell'. 'Blue Bell'? Who would have guessed?

"Nothing to say?" Her velvety words came out rather brassy. Aye, the blue devil was back – Joe couldn't help himself. One minute she's like a sweet, innocent, little girl; the next minute she's like a wee brat, an audacious one! Did this girl have two people inside of her, battling it out, he thought extremely upset. He was just about to leave, when she hastily jumped up, and almost pushed him gently back into his seat.

"I'm sorry. I'm sorry," she pleaded profusely with him to sit back down and just "please just give me a chance, one more chance." Joe could swear that he saw tears in her fired-up blue eyes. At long last, he settled down and this time, he did not have to pretend to give her a disgruntled look. He just gave it!

Never in his life, had he felt this way about someone, *and* so strongly. He usually doused all those problematic and annoying feelings with his trusty liquor. It always did the trick, but now, not only did he have to feel them, he also had to deal with them. He almost felt sorry for himself. Where was a drink when he needed it?

"Here you go," Cathy has returned with their good-looking food. She also remembered about Pup. With her usual warm smiles and a promise of a refill, Cathy left them, once more.

Joe took a sip from his deep cup and imagined with all his might, that the strong black stuff was actually his favourite drink. 'Blue-girl' was still looking at him pleadingly, her whole face pulled into a puppy's expression when it wanted something; she looked so sad, so miserable, so pitiful.

Should he feel sorry for her? No! She should be the one apologising *and* she should be the one feeling sorry for HIM! Joe looked down at his food, it looked so good. What a pity that his appetite was now lost between all his jumbled-up emotions, dare he say feelings.

"My name is Blue Bell," she said softly in the friendliest tone he had ever heard. "I know it is a funny name, very unusual, but it's a long story and you probably don't want to hear it. Not now, anyway." Again she looked at him, but this time he saw not only her previous pleadings, but also blue eyes filled with fear.

This puzzled Joe; why would she be afraid? Was she perhaps afraid of him? He took another sip, again trying his imagine-a-drink trick. It didn't work, unfortunately. So he guessed that he would have to play nice.

"I probably do want to hear..." he tested the unsure waters carefully. She was afraid of him (he assumed), he was afraid of her (she was a human after all!). Where did that leave them, he wondered as he heard his stomach rumble – his appetite was back, with a vengeance.

Blue Bell laughed, she also heard and immediately delved into her garden salad, as if she was asking and giving permission to eat. Joe didn't waste any time joining her in the ritual of eating.

Through mouthfuls of food, Blue Bell – Joe happened to like that name, it was way better than 'Blue-girl' – explained where, or rather how she got her name. It was actually quite simple, Joe learned, Blue Bell obviously wasn't her real name. *She* chose this name purposely to spite her mother. She wouldn't say why, nor what her real name was. Ahh, Joe thought silently, he was rather looking forward to discovering that truth about her.

In between big bites, greasy ones and leafy ones, 'Cave-man' Joe and 'Blue-girl' Blue Bell, slowly but surely started to get to know each other. Slowly and cautiously, they did.

CHAPTER SIX

Three days later, and they were flying it on their journey north. Joe was quite pleased with the headway they were making – even if it was the long way home – headway, not only on the road, but also between them.

He discovered that Blue Bell was actually a nice girl, with a nice temperament. The bright blue hair and her entirely black accoutrement was all just a ploy to throw people off. So, in a sense, she was exactly like him; avoiding people. The only difference, they used different methods of achieving their goal, to avoid people.

Joe was trekking through a quiet part of town. As usual, Casey was sleeping on Blue Bell's lap. She was lost in the scenery, it would appear. "Did you know that my brother has passed away?" she asked, still transfixed by the new scenery. "Yes, he died a few months ago," she turned her head slowly towards him.

Joe could see and hear the sadness, she tried very hard to play down. At first, he didn't know what to say, but then it was like a light went on inside of him, and he, Joe, suddenly knew what to say. "Your brother Casey?" he hovered over each word and hoped that he had asked his question as gently as he possibly could, being a cave-man and all that.

"Yes, Casey..." she sighed, looking down at Pup. He was making faint snoring sounds – this pup could sleep! Her thin mouth twisted funny, as if she couldn't decide between smiling and crying. Joe felt sorry for her; he even considered pulling off the road. This felt like a face-to-face conversation. He knew that he had to put some emotion into it.

He started slowing down, put his indicator on... "What are you doing?" she asked, frowning deeply. She almost sounded panicked. Aye, Joe thought, I'm scaring her off again. He increased his speed and eventually she relaxed a bit. This side was new to him; it felt like those two people battling it out, all over again. He had really hoped that it was all behind them now, that somehow the two of them had clicked in their own unique way!

Was he wrong? Was she even more broken than he suspected? It looked like Joe wasn't getting anything else, anything more out of her, at least not now. So, they sat in silence, again, staring this way and that way.

She wasn't talking, her blue hair formed the perfect curtain between them as she rested her head against her window, and he wasn't equipped well enough, dealing with people, dealing with their fragile emotions... it was almost too much for him... but he kept his cool. After all, he had offered the ride *and* he had two souls to take into account.

It was late in the afternoon, when Joe and Blue Bell

stood waiting for Casey to do his thing. The wee fella urgently had to go. So, here they stood, Nancy parked safely behind them, just gazing into the dull red of the striking sunset. Both enjoyed the view, the spectacular view. Joe, in all his life, never grew tired of a beautiful sunset, especially this one which painted everything red, even the rock canyon beneath them. He could have sworn that, had there been any water down there, it too would have been red, red like the glorious sun.

Even Blue Bell's hair had a red tint to it. Joe laughed, he didn't know that it was possible to outvie that brilliant bright blue.

Blue Bell looked at him curiously. After all this time, and she still could not pin Joe. She could tell that he was decent under that rough exterior – especially when he wore his red-and-white bandanna – but with Joe, came some baggage. Maybe even a lot, but make no mistake, he was a good guy in his own Joe-way. There just wasn't enough time for her to fully understand and appreciate him. Their time was too little for building a proper relationship. Blue Bell had this inkling that had they more time together, Joe could have been her 'new' Casey, but their trip would end soon, and that would be that.

"It's so beautiful, so peaceful out here," she observed carried away, "it can make you forget a lot of things." It felt as though she could be carried away by it all, to a better place, hopefully.

"How true," Joe assented to her observation. This young girl had insight that few younglings had. She once again, reminded Joe of his daughter. Was that what attracted him to this young girl? This blue-haired, one-of-a-kind. He glanced at her furtively. She looked so happy, her thin lips were pulled back in a smile, even her blue eyes appeared content. Her blue hair fluttered lightly, quietly in the gentle mountain breeze. It almost looked like a commercial, like they were trying to sell happiness in a bizarre way.

Joe smiled at his peculiar thought.

"I see Casey is finally finished. Do you want to stay a few more minutes?" he enquired delicately. Sometimes the balance, her balance wasn't quite there yet, and the last thing he wanted, was to upset that balance, upset her!

"We can go. I've seen enough," she answered very blasé and turned away from the mystifying view. With Casey safe in her covered arms, she headed for Nancy, Joe's faithful truck.

Joe believed that it was moments like these that made everything worthwhile, every little... hump and bump, and he also believed that these moments would help Blue Bell tremendously, it was like silent therapy. These moments held some sort of magic, he couldn't quite explain it, but he most definitely felt it!

That night they visited another diner, Dot's Diner. The name flashed brightly and invitingly. Again, Joe found the perfect spot for his massive blue-and-silver Rig. Nancy would be pleased, he thought as the three of them headed inside.

This diner was rather quiet; probably due to the sudden cold and the late hour. Joe wanted to push hard on this last stretch of their journey. He somehow felt, oddly enough, hot-footed to get home. He could not explain it, but that was how he felt, hot-footed. Joe started toiling anew about home and about going home. He often imagined what that would be like.

Normally not for long, because his fears and his reclusiveness would always get the better of him, Joe Mountain.

"This table looks good," Blue Bell announced and immediately flopped down on the plastic covered bench. She took Casey out of her jet-black jacket, and gently placed him next to her. He sat quietly as he inspected his new surroundings. His little nose and fluffy ears worked overtime.

Joe took the seat opposite them and made his slightly overweight and bulky frame comfortable. He looked for menus, but there were none to be found. Blue Bell tried to entertain the pup while they waited for some service. Joe couldn't be sure, but he had this feeling that she was on the fritz again. Aye, he sure as hell hoped that, that wasn't the case. They still had a long way to go...

"Evenin' folks. Would you like to hear our midnight specials?" Joe hadn't even noticed the cutest waitress he has ever seen, standing next to him. She looked like a Barbie-doll, complete with faded blonde hair and baby-blue eyes. He completely forgot her question... midnight specials... he didn't know that they even existed, midnight specials. Imagine that... "Midnight specials, you say," buying himself some time, "what are those?"

'Barbie-doll' smiled brightly and in the cutest voice she rattled off their midnight specials. Joe almost forgot to pay attention, he was so fixated on her tiny, shiny mouth.

"I'll have the special with the twist," Blue Bell answered dryly. "You can also bring my coffee in a mug, thanks," she added. It sounded a lot like a command. Joe grew even more concerned about Blue

Bell's emotional well-being. He shuddered inside.

"You can make that two," he told their waitress while holding up two fingers. He even gave a smile, just to show that they weren't completely screwed up. Joe considered having a scald; coffee would just keep him awake. "A cup of tea would be fine, thank you," again flashing his pearlies. He stuffed his bandanna in his jacket's pocket as 'Barbie-doll' left with their simple order. It was warm inside the modern diner. Having extra meat also didn't hurt.

"Are you all right?" Joe finally dared asking Blue Bell that delayed question. He kept putting it off hoping that it wouldn't be necessary, but now, it would seem, that it was justified and his timing was also justified. He secretly and quietly hoped that she would confirm that she was all right, because then, he wouldn't have to delve into her emotions, into her inner world, with her!

She stayed silent for a minute or two, as if she was weighing her options.

"Would it matter if I were?" she answered with a question. She hardly looked at him; this worried Joe even more. What was he to do? What was he to say? He was no therapist. What did he know about heads, anyway? It only made his head hurt, and now, he had to deal with this, with her, without any liquor! Aye!

He counted his next words carefully, and then counted them again, until finally, 'Barbie-doll' arrived with their hot beverages. Probably no liquor in that, he thought disheartened.

After unloading their drinks and hot milk, "Barbie-doll' informed them that their food was almost ready, and again left with an adorable smile. Joe wished that they could switch places. Even that, dealing with strangers, would be less scary than facing this fickle, erratic, blue-haired young'un!

"Are you finished?" she asked while reaching for the sugar. Joe hadn't realized that he was stuck on the sugar. He immediately passed it on to Blue Bell.

"Can I have your saucer?" she asked again, a bit like a robot. With a huge frown, he handed her his white saucer. She carefully poured warm milk from the petite jug, into his saucer. She then swirled it around just as carefully, and finally she set it down gently beside Casey.

He was very pleased with his lick of the creamy, warm milk. He messed a bit, but Blue Bell wiped it clean without delay. She tickled his belly when he finished, which caused her to laugh. Maybe not whole-heartedly, but laugh, she did.

Joe answered with a relieved smile. Thank heavens, for Pup; he always could make her laugh with his little-dog-body and his little-dog-noises. He was glad that they had such a good connection, let the pup do, what the human cannot!

'Barbie-doll' came walking down the aisle, almost like a fairy, with her delicate hands full. "One for you, and one for you," singing her words as she placed their warm plates before them. "Will there be anything else?" she asked proudly with her perfect smile. Her blue eyes waiting patiently, brightly.

"No, thank you. This looks mighty good." Again, Joe stared at the cute, Barbie-faced waitress. Very pleased, she nodded, she spun around, and danced away to the big front counter.

Joe shook his head in amazement. It must be nice to be so free, free to express yourself, any which way you want to. The only thing that ever freed him, was his bottle, his damn liquor. No human could do that, not even himself.

He did feel free in Nancy, but was he really free?

"This is really good," Blue Bell remarked with her dainty mouth fully stuffed.

Joe could barely make out what she was saying. He assumed that it must've been good, because she was smiling now with bulging cheeks, the tanned skin, stretched thinly over each bulge.

Joe couldn't help himself, he started shaking with laughter, and before he knew it, he was bellowing with laughter. It was rolling out of him like a giant wave. A giant wave of relief and a giant wave of nervousness.

All tension gone, all tension released.

At last, Joe could eat, he could enjoy himself.

CHAPTER SEVEN

They were hitting the road again. Nancy was eating up the asphalt, making quick work of the many miles. Joe had the radio on and was humming happily to one of his favourite tunes. Even Blue Bell, made inarticulate sounds every so often.

All three were feeling really pumped-up, until they saw the sign.

The sign.

That sign meant that they were going home; he was going home.

That sign meant that his life would change, one way or another, irrevocably.

That sign meant that Blue Bell was stepping off, quite possibly, for good. Stepping off and stepping out of his life. She would leave a big gaping hole in his heart – this blue-haired angel had grown on him, quietly and swiftly.

Joe sniffed. He pretended to sneeze. He couldn't afford to show his real emotion. That was a sure way to get hurt, and without his trusty liquor, it would leave him vulnerable. Joe didn't want to go down that road again – it was bloody awful!

Why was he going home again, he alarmingly asked himself.

Unfortunately, it was too late to turn back, or to even turn any other way. Blue Bell accepted this ride, because he was headed north...

"Can you stop at that filling station?" she asked abruptly, a bit uninspired. Joe looked at her, quickly. He could feel worries starting to work their way into his brain. Soon he would be deeply unsettled. Aye, everything was going so well... Blue Bell just started trusting him. She told him about her brother, Casey, the full story. She also told him about her difficult mother and her unyielding ways. She made life, really tough for Blue Bell, especially after her brother's death.

Casey was the one who understood her, and her illness. He was the one that came up with ingenious ways for her to cope, not only with life, but also with her mother. He was also, sadly, the only one who was always there for her, even in her maddest moments when things were really tough, Casey was there – like a real-life hero.

Joe parked his blue-and-silver Rig, far out of the way, and waited for 'Blue-girl' (he sometimes, still called her that) to get out, and do whatever it was that she wanted to do.

Blue Bell turned all the way towards him. Pup turned with. She felt all kinds of emotions running through her, almost like a locomotive on steroids. This man, 'Cave-man', has been so good to her. He didn't have to be, but he was. He was probably closer to her these past few days than anyone, anyone alive that is. She'll miss him, rusticity and all!

She knew that deep down there was a good, good heart.

"I'll be right back," she finally said, "have to use the lady's room." With that she lifted little Casey into Joe's man-sized hands, and quickly jumped out before he could say or do anything.

He watched her disappear into the tiny rest rooms, and then turned his focus back to Casey. He must be hungry, Joe thought, growing at that pace, will do that to a dog. He'll check to see...

Bzzz, bzzz. Bzzz, bzzz. What was that, he wondered. His eye caught a slim phone, a bright blue one, on Blue Bell's seat. It was vibrating in concert with the buzzing. Joe hesitated for a moment or two, then picked up the silent cell phone. He didn't know why he did, he just did.

He glanced at the screen, trying hard not to read anything. But this message, he could not ignore. In glowing letters across the cell phone's face were displayed the following words: Where are you?

Just that single line: Where are you? Just that one question: Where are you?

Immediately, Joe questioned who it was from. Was it her mother, a boyfriend perhaps? He didn't know and thus decided to return her phone to its earlier resting place. Casey almost looked as baffled as he did. Joe hadn't noticed the minutes flying by.

He was replaying her words in his uneasy mind.

"I was thirteen when I first noticed that I was very different from other kids my age. It seemed that they all had good, solid foundations. That they knew where they were going in life; they had clarity. I didn't.

My world was always shaky, in flux. I could never understand why. Why were their lives so simple? Why was mine so extremely complicated, so intense, and so confusing?

At first, I couldn't make head or tail about my life, especially the hidden one. The one nobody ever saw. They didn't even know that it existed, let alone understood it. My brother, Casey, was the only one who knew, and who understood, fully. He understood not only my life, my illness, but me! Me!

That changed everything, everything. Except for my mother... she was harder and colder than stone. She didn't understand a thing! She didn't even try to!"

Joe understood that Blue Bell had a rough life, specifically after Casey's death. She also told him how he died. It was the weirdest thing...

One day, he went hiking, without Blue Bell, and never came back! A few days later, he returned as if nothing happened, as if it was the most normal thing in the world. Everyone questioned him, Blue Bell most of all, but all they got was an "I don't remember." That was all.

Blue Bell was sick with worry, and of course this meant nothing good for her illness. There was nothing she could do.

"Shortly after his return, Casey fell ill, without any warning. We thought that his mysterious disappearance was bad, this was even worse!

His body deteriorated at such a fast rate, three days later, there was no more Casey."

Those words were devastatingly harsh. Joe could still see her delicate face before him; it was riddled with pain and heartache. She told him that right after, she fell into a deep depression, the deepest one yet.

There was a time when she thought that she would never get out of that dark, morbid place. Day in and day out, everything was covered in black, the darkest of black.

"It was not until I had my meltdown, that I remained trapped in my own, private hell – a black hell. My mother was fed-up with me and my precious feelings. That was what she called it, 'my precious feelings.' She could not comprehend that on top of my hellish, troublesome mood swings, I also had to deal with Casey's death. Try dealing with that from emotional extremes that you can't even imagine, which yo-yoed you all day long. That was hell, with a capital 'h'!"

Joe finally understood what Blue Bell was doing in his truck. According to her, her monstrous mother had kicked her out. "She couldn't stand living with this fucked-up child, any longer, with her irritating moodiness; fickle nature; short-tempered spoiled brat; gloomy; mopy, you name it, I have been called that and much worse!"

And that was that...

"Dear God!" he exclaimed loudly. He thought that he had it rough...

He stopped abruptly and checked his watch. Was it his imagination or was Blue Bell taking unusually long? He couldn't be sure. He didn't check the time when they had stopped, and he was so completely absorbed by her story, he simply lost track of time.

Casey gave a high-pitched bark, his first, as if he was feeling the same as Joe. Joe patted him proudly on his little head. The wee fella was getting big. But more importantly, where was Blue Bell? What was taking so long? Joe could feel himself freaking out a bit; apparently he wasn't the only one looking for her, and that was exactly what he did – he went looking for her,

'Blue-girl'.

Joe searched every inch of the filling station, every inch. Neither he, nor Pup, could find Blue Bell anywhere. Where the hell was she, he asked himself for the umpteenth time. His 'freaking out just a bit', has turned into full-blown panic by now. He felt responsible for her, and if anything, anything, happened to her, he would probably... simply put, there would not be a pub big enough to douse what he was feeling and thinking right now!

"Where are you, Blue Bell?" he asked audibly. He didn't care if anyone heard; he was too disturbed to care. All he wanted, was to find 'Blue-girl'. He racked his brains for where she might be, then he had his light-bulb-moment. How could he be so dense?

Joe raced back to his truck, and efficiently fast opened the door and jumped in. He reached for her blue cell phone – where are you? He finally remembered the message on her phone.

Her phone!

There would definitely be contact numbers on, clues!

Phew, he thought relieved and immediately started looking through her contact list. Casey watched his every move with great interest, turning his wee head, this way and that way. His dark-brown eyes were locked on Joe's big fingers swiping through loads of information.

After a while, Joe still couldn't find any clues, anything relevant, but he kept going – there must be something. Something, no matter how small, no matter how insignificant. He will find it, Joe decided determinedly.

Still nothing, nothing so far that is, but he once again, kept going, swiping away at her smart phone. Casey kept watching – you could almost see the frown on his furry forehead as he concentrated.

Joe was just about to give up, when his tired green eyes caught a smiley. He had missed it the first time. He could see why – it was well hidden among other images. Joe took a better look at the yellow smiley. It was a yellow, smiling face, and even with his glasses on, he could barely make out the initials on it. "JC," he read aloud. He wondered what they stood for. There were no other clues hinting to her whereabouts, not even one clarifying the mysterious 'JC' initials.

With Blue Bell's phone resting quietly in his pocket, and Casey sitting very alert on the too big, passenger seat, Joe could, at long last, take to the road again, and this time he went in search of an eatery. Not a blue-haired runaway.

CHAPTER EIGHT

This time, Joe did not stop at a diner. This time, he stopped at a local food truck parked next to the highway. He pulled up, right next to it; he liked having Nancy close by. The food truck seemed like a good idea, seeing that he was one short and he had to take care of dear Casey.

He bought a proper cheeseburger with fries and a large Coke, he was extremely thirsty. He also didn't care about all that sugar right now. He just wanted some comfort. Hopefully, he would also be able to think more clearly on a full stomach.

He and Casey shared the 'too much for one' meal; Joe seated on a wooden bench, and little Casey sitting on the ground next to him. He ate every morsel with great enthusiasm, and then begged for more. Joe just stared in amazement at this little guy's appetite, and not even mentioning his little beggar-face – he had never seen anything like it before!

Joe continued feeding little Pup while taking a bite every so often. He used his large Coke to wash down his very last mouthful. He could feel his belly popping out – that was a... lot... of... food, he thought with a big grin on his face. He rubbed his full belly satisfiedly as he leaned back. He could not help but notice Casey's little bump. It was obvious that the wee fella *had* enough to eat.

Bzzz, bzzz. Bzzz, bzzz. Joe felt Blue Bell's cell vibrating in his pocket. He was nearly too afraid to look. Him, being afraid of a wee phone!

Bloody hell!

Joe exaggeratedly took out her blue cell phone and fearlessly looked at the lit screen. He did not need his glasses for this message – it was exactly the same as the first one: Where are you??

The only difference, this familiar line had two question marks!

The message only displayed a number, and no name. Once more, Joe had questions about the sender – who had sent it? – but no answers. This frustrated him greatly. He thought he knew Blue Bell well enough; it would seem that he only knew the tip of the Blue Iceberg.

Joe wondered about his next move. He wasn't quite sure what to do next, in fact, he wasn't at all sure!

This left him feeling helpless; a feeling he wasn't particularly fond of. And to cap everything, he had no help from his alcohol friend. He would have to do everything alone, *and* he would have to do it without his trusty liquor – no Band-aid for Joe, no protective buffer for Joe.

"Poor me," he first thought and then made his pitiful words audible. He wiped his forehead with his red-and-white bandanna, disturbing some of his wavy brown hair, capturing some of the moisture. All this, was beginning to give him a mighty headache, *and* this was only the beginning...

He grabbed a confused Casey and hoisted them both up into his beloved Nancy, before Joe Mountain could change his mind, before he could become Joe Coward.

Joe was driving along a familiar main route, keeping an eye out for 'Blue-girl' – you never know, she may very well be just around the next bend.

Joe knew that if he continued on this road, *he* would be home soon; what a scary and unsettling thought. Huh! Joe also knew that he could dial the number and finally find out who had sent the multiple messages. But he sensed that if he did that, he – Joe Mountain – would step into some nastiness he would much rather avoid. He had enough on his delicate plate, and balancing everything, became increasingly harder, the closer he got to his destination.

He looked over at Pup. The wee fella was resting peacefully with only his tiny, brown ears and his tiny, black nose twitching. His cropful belly was speaking loudly. Joe smiled, at least there was this little ray of sunshine in his troublesome, sometimes dark, life.

Joe felt extremely nervous, almost to the point of pulling over and looking disgustedly and sickly at his late lunch. This maddened him; why on earth, would he, a grown man and all, after all this time, still feel *this* way? And so strongly?

His green eyes answered in kind and he narrowed them with a deep prominent frown. Joe had serious doubts about returning home. Serious doubts. With every familiar street and every familiar building, he just wanted to point Nancy's huge nose in a different direction, but strangely enough, something kept him from doing exactly that – to run like his pants were on fire.

With the familiar terrain, came very familiar feelings. Also, familiar memories; the ones he could actually, remember. Joe had to admit, not all his memories were bad; there were some pretty good ones, in there as well. Depending on his mood, he remembered either the good, or the bad, and sometimes, the two were so muddled, he couldn't be sure which was which. So, he just remembered everything *or* nothing, again, depending on his mood, which was all over the place these past few days!

Sometimes, it felt like a 'Lucky Packet' inside of him; he didn't always know what he was going to get next: the good, the bad, or perhaps, both!

So in essence, it wasn't really a 'Lucky' packet, it was just what he called it, an unplumbable 'Lucky Packet', and it resided within Joe Mountain...

Blue Bell walked as fast as her young legs would go. She had to get away. She just had to!

She hoped, maybe foolishly, that Joe would understand, but realistically speaking, how could he. How could he possibly understand? How? Not even Casey, bless his soul, could, and he really tried. In all fairness, he did understand all her ups and downs, but not fully. Blue Bell finally realised that the only one who did understand, was Blue Bell herself. That was just one more reason for her to be alone, completely and utterly alone. No one, not even her own mother, could understand or fully comprehend the depth of her illness. They just couldn't. And although it was an illness according to the professionals, it was her life, actually a way of life for her. That was how she lived, and no one understood this. No one... that was why she had to get away, as far away as possible.

Joe had helped her this far, but now, she would have to go the rest of the way, all alone.

Blue Bell did feel bad about the way she had ditched Joe and poor Casey. But there was no other way, there just wasn't. She sat, her head filled with all these cumbersome thoughts, but what else could she do. It had to be done!

It has only been a few hours and already she was missing Pup aka Casey. She felt glad that, at least, she got to name him – now, he has a proper name and one he can be proud of, for it belonged to the one person, she cared about most in the world. And that said a lot.

Blue Bell sat quietly on the bus; the bus that would take her where she wanted to be, where she needed to be. Luckily, Joe paid for all their meals, so she had just enough cash for her ticket, her one-way ticket. For where she was going, there was no coming back, *and* she wasn't planning on coming back.

Why would she?

Her brother was dead, and her mother was a lost cause, according to her. Besides *she* kicked her out. That also meant kicking Blue Bell out of her life.

On some weird level, that hurt, that actually hurt, Blue Bell thought. But why, why does it hurt, she asked herself knowing that the answer was either buried deep inside, or so obvious, she just chose to ignore it. Either way, it didn't really matter. Not now, anyway. She just wondered, that's all!

The bus moved slowly through the city, through the busy streets. Blue Bell didn't really know this city, this part of America. But she has seen pictures, and on those pictures it looked good, good enough for her to disappear. That was why she chose this city. It would be easy for her to get lost and alone, in this city, even with her electrifying blue hair.

The blue hair and the usual black clothing assured... it guaranteed her solitude. That was exactly what she wanted: solitude, to be alone.

No more hassles, from no one! For the getting lost part, the moment Blue Bell stepped off the bus, she did disappear, into an army of coloured hair, into an army of freaks!

That was why she chose *this* city – this city of freaks...

CHAPTER NINE

Joe turned the corner. He turned the familiar corner slowly, like a snail looking for a parking spot. It wasn't that difficult to manoeuvre his Big Rig; he has been doing it for so long. Besides, he and Nancy understood each other, very well.

It was a pity that he didn't understand people that well, or even got along that well. But hey, that was life, for him anyway. Joe shrugged, he had accepted that about himself, about life, about his lot. Aye, now he was getting too philosophical, and that on an empty sober stomach! He had to decide, now, whether he was just passing through, *or* actually stopping. He knew that stopping would change everything. Every part of his life, his entire life. That scared him, a lot. He felt like he was having a panic attack as the seconds ticked by. Tick-tick, tick-tick. What was he going to do... tick-tick... what... tick-tick...? "I can't breathe," he whispered in a tight voice.

He glanced wide-eyed at poor Casey next to him. He could feel Joe's panic, and nervously, restlessly moved about on the large seat. This pup must be psychic, Joe thought in a moment of clarity.

And that was all he needed! A moment of clarity!

He immediately picked up speed and tried to take in as much as he possibly could while passing by the very familiar, too familiar, house with the big, red pot sitting on the porch.

Joe could finally flee these familiar surroundings, this part of his life and of course, those sticky and extremely unpleasant, accompanying feelings.

Aye, those feelings. He could breathe more easily now. He really did not expect such a strong, severe reaction.

All he wanted, was to go home. What now? He wondered defeatedly, and for a brief second reconsidered going back, but he immediately accelerated. He really did not feel up to it; facing his past, his home, his loved ones. Joe just wasn't game for it; it would seem that he, Joe Mountain, was not ready to go home!

He pointed Nancy's nose in the opposite direction, and just kept going, and going. He secretly hoped that he would run out of road, because then, he would really have to make a decision, *and* stick to it, no matter what. All this, this casting about, was making him sick, and not just physically.

Blue Bell discovered that blending in, was remarkably easy, and easy for her. She had thought that there might be a slight chance of her sticking out like a sore thumb. No such luck. Here, she was just one more, one more of many. Many freaks, many weirdo's, many eccentrics.

It was still early, so there was enough time for her to find a place to crash. The idea wasn't to be homeless, so she had to act fast, or else, she would be labelled as such.

She started looking around attentively – that was the fastest way to study your environment, and it was also a sure way of finding some lucky, perhaps unlucky (depending on your vantage point), turd to take her, the sweet innocent, but troubled teen, in. You found those motherly-hens, everywhere. You just had to know where to look, and how to look; Blue Bell, did this well, very well!

She thought of Joe... shook her blue head, trying to shake the image loose, and moved on. There wasn't any time for that; playing someone, took time, and *she* had to use hers wisely.

So, she started searching, searching, searching for that right one... was that her? Blue Bell intensified her focus and zoomed in on this friendly-looking, unsuspecting woman across the street. The middle-aged woman stood looking at arrangements of flowers. Flowers... that was it!

Blue Bell had found her target.

"Are those sunflowers?" a young voice asked. The woman turned around. It took her a few seconds to reply, appropriately.

"Yes, those are sunflowers. Why?" she answered as politely as she could. The young girl looked straight at her. This made her a bit uncomfortable.

The next moment, a wide smile appeared across her tanned face. She cocked her head to one side, and said sweetly, "I like yellow. And they remind me of the sun."

Her bright, blue hair fell over her covered shoulder as she cocked her head again.

The woman just stared in amazement. She didn't know what to make of this youngster. She knew that teens tend to be a bit whimsical, but this one, this one took eccentricity to a whole new level.

"Do you work here?" the girl asked innocently, hoping that she wasn't being too forward, or anything. She had noticed the woman's green apron.

"No, this here, is my flower shop," the woman answered proudly and precisely, very to the point. She studied the young girl before her, even more closely. Apart from the wild-blue hair, she had the most delicate face the woman had ever seen. Even her blue eyes seemed gentle, unlike her wavy, wild blue hair. The jet-black clothes she wore, could not even hide her petite build. It was just as petite as her petite facial features.

"You have a nice shop," she remarked as they proceeded inside. The woman was actually busy with a rather important order, but she chose to listen even so. Maybe, there was more to this strange-looking girl than meets the eye, she thought and continued as naturally and as normally as she could manage.

"I really like it," she complimented as she twirled around and around, trying to get a good look at the crowded, little flower shop. "Have you had this shop long?" the girl asked looking genuinely interested.

The woman still had difficulty trying to assess whether this youngster was really interested, or just feigning, being up to no good. Taking into account her past, then this type of behaviour, this type of thinking was not surprising, the woman thought sourly. Her past, was not a pretty one. It was in fact a hard one,

one of the hardest you can find...

"What are you making?" The young girl leaned over her shoulder to get a better look. Her shiny, blue hair fell over part of her tanned face as she did so.

The woman stepped aside, partly so that the teen could get a better look, but mostly, she wasn't used to people, strangers getting so close, especially ones with funny-looking hair.

She looked her over, once more, again trying to uncover her true motive for standing in her shop, a flower shop, no less! "I'm making bouquets for a baby-shower," she paused for a moment, "I know, a baby-shower." The woman added that last part in an effort to elicit more of the young girl's answers, perhaps then, she would be able to know for sure.

"They are beautiful. So colourful, even the..." The woman smiled, very pleased – it worked. The young girl was talking rapidly now, without any encouragement.

After awhile of back-and-forth patter, the woman concluded that it was safe talking to the blue-haired stranger in her shop.

Blue Bell couldn't believe her luck. Here she was walking home with Maizey, the woman from the flower shop. She couldn't believe how easy that was – she most definitely, still had her touch. Wow! She exclaimed inwardly, feeling very smug over her victory. All she had to do now, was to play along for the time being. Until, she felt that she had her – hook, line and sinker.

Blue Bell knew that it sounded cruel, and it probably was, but what was she supposed to do? She was kicked out unexpectedly and rudely, to put it mildly. She had no other choice, and to top things off, she had this terrible disease to contend with, *and* she had to do so, all by herself!

They neared a house, her house, Blue Bell assumed, because it was the very last house on that street. Next to it, was an open field with a few trees sticking out here and there before the green forest began.

She turned her attention back to Maizey's house. It was, what you would call, a story-book house. The house itself wasn't huge, but the way it was presented – it took Blue Bell's breath away. She had never seen anything like it, in her entire life.

The home (it wasn't really a house, it was more a home!) matched the story-book garden, perfectly. She let her blue eyes glide over the fantasy garden – it boasted every colour under the sun, maybe even every flower. Who knew? Blue Bell fully understood why this woman had a flower shop. She could clearly see her passion not only for flowers, but also for every plant growing in that garden. It was like she had charmed every single flower into a radiant, vibrant blooming version of itself.

Blue Bell was actually speechless.

"Magnificent, aren't they?" Maizey filled the silence with her own words of praise. "This garden here, it's more than just a garden. It's my very own piece of paradise; my pride and joy."

"I can see that," Blue Bell finally answered the woman who stood mesmerized by her own handiwork, almost as if she was one with it. This made Blue Bell sit upright, figuratively speaking. Maybe Maizey wasn't just a boring pudding. Maybe there was more than meets the eye, she thought a bit unnerved, her overconfidence waning a bit.

"Come inside, Blue Bell," the enigmatic woman invited her in warmly, "otherwise, you'll stand there all day long." She laughed unexpectedly, filling every corner of the magical garden with her infectious, pleasant laughter.

Blue Bell felt her overconfidence, waning a bit more. Was she on top?

She had second-thoughts, though not serious, she had second-thoughts – what has she gotten herself into, or was it perhaps, WHO?

CHAPTER TEN

Joe kept on going, and going, further than he wanted to, but he didn't go back South – that was a plus, a huge plus. It meant that Joe wasn't as afraid as he had first thought. It would seem that there was a very strong possibility, that he would go home and face his past, *and* everyone in it.

These illuminating thoughts kept meandering through his psyche, over and over again. It was almost like a Joe-revelation, he thought proudly and sighed a sweet sigh of relief. Things were not as bad as he had thought, believed really. Joe smiled more comfortably, more relaxed at little Pup. The wee fella still missed Blue Bell.

"Aye," he sighed again, aloud this time, "that Blue one." Joe wondered more than once, whether he'd ever see her again. He had no answers to that, but he guessed that time would tell. Hopefully, it would tell him, all he needed to know... why did she leave? ... what happened to her? ... basically it would give him closure to this Blue Chapter in his life.

Joe suddenly frowned, deeply; was that the reason for him wanting to go home? So that Joe Mountain could finally have closure...

It would sure put a stop to all those haunting thoughts he had, had lately.

All the memories... the tough memories...

For a moment he got lost, but then immediately regained control. He quickly reminded himself of where he was headed. He couldn't take a chance; he knew full well, that to get lost in his past, in those memories would or could cause him to turn to the liquor again, *and* he could not, would not afford that. He worked so hard getting to this point in his life; he wasn't at all willing to give that up, or to abandon his sobriety.

He was in fact searching for decent accommodation for him and Pup, *and* his massive Nancy, before all this nonsense started. "Bloody hell," he said softly, "bloody hell." He wasn't one who usually swore!

Lucky enough, the next section of road held a promising-looking, pink motel.

"Can I have a room please?" Joe asked plainly. He was able to park his Rig nearby, and in a good-looking spot. Feeling at ease, he patiently waited for the shuffling old man to do the transaction, and hand him his keys, which was on a pink key-ring.

Joe stood looking at the pink key-ring while hovering at his appointed door. The pink somehow reminded him of 'Blue-girl' – why was that, he wondered as he put the key in the awaiting keyhole.

He stepped into a small and cosy room. If you didn't have a home, he thought longingly, then this would be it: your home, although temporary.

He laid Pup on the bed – he was fast asleep – and started investigating every nook and cranny. It was just like him to do that – looking everywhere, on top, way down low. He called it Joe's way, seeing that he was very particular about where and how he rested his dark brown curly-head.

Pleasingly satisfied that everything checked out, Joe looked for something to read. Joe loved to read, ever since he could remember, he loved to read – it was just a pity that he didn't have nearly enough time for that.

"Hmm," Joe expressed, totally absorbed in thought, "The Holy Bible." He sat down slowly, partly to not disturb Pup, and also he was flabbergasted for finding only a Bible to read. Not even a magazine! Nonetheless, he took out his reading-glasses and started flipping through the extremely thin pages.

Some of it looked familiar, some not so familiar, and the rest – which happened to be the bulk of it – definitely not!

Joe kept on paging through the heavy, thick black book. He had to kill some time, otherwise dinner would not be dinner.

"Leviticus... Joshua... Ezra..." he read aloud, "Psalms... Isaiah," he read further. "Oh, this looks promising. Daniel. Hmm. Let's have a look..." Pup was sitting upright now, pricking up his tiny ears as he listened attentively to Joe's continuous murmuring. He was reading through some of the Bible passages.

"Hmm," he stopped briefly and looked at Pup as if to say 'pay attention Casey,' "listen to this..." Pup turned his multicoloured face towards Joe and looked cute as a button, doing so. He reached out and scratched Pup behind his fluffy ears. Pup loved that, he even made tiny groaning noises to show his satisfaction.

Joe gave him a chummy smile and a chummy pat on his head, before he pushed his glasses back for some more reading. What was he reading again? Oh, yea, the Bible, he thought silently – "Where was I?" He posed the question rather to Pup than himself. It still felt funny reading the Bible, especially after so many years.

His long finger finally found the passage he was looking for. He first read it silently, and then, after a brief interval, he read the whole passage aloud to his only 'non-paying' listener – "Daniel four, verse five." Joe cleared his throat, and in his best minister's voice, he read the whole, relevant verse aloud, complete with mimicked hand gestures.

"I saw a dream which made me afraid, and the thoughts upon my bed and the visions of my head troubled me."

He read further, "Therefore made I a decree to bring in all the wise [men] of Babylon before me, that they might make known unto me the interpretation of the dream."

He looked over at Pup, checking to see if he was still paying attention. Satisfied that he was, Joe read even further.

"Then came in the magicians, the astrologers, the Chaldeans, and the soothsayers: and I told the dream before them; but they did not make known unto me the interpretation thereof."

Joe slowly lowered the heavy book and it came to rest on his big lap. He just stared in front of him for a few seconds, his light frame balancing on the tip of his gnome-like nose. His green eyes started moving slowly in their sockets. He lifted his bulky arm a tad bit, absentmindedly and combed his large fingers through his brown curly hair, touching his red-and-white bandanna briefly.

After reading the whole passage aloud, especially the first verse, Joe could feel... something... something in him click, it finally clicked. And it felt so real, Joe could almost hear it click. Who would have thought that reading from the Bible (The Holy Bible), just one passage, could have such an effect, and so rapidly? Joe had this recurring thought, circling him like a hungry lion.

He was still taken aback by its intensity – was it the Bible or was it the click itself? He wondered again, and then with his arms up in the air, concluded that it was both, definitely both!

He looked at Pup who was still watching him with full concentration. His tiny ears still pricked up, his dark brown eyes opened wide. Aye, Joe knew at long last, what to do *and* how to do it, but before he could act, he needed to feed this little Jack Russell.

Blue Bell passed a big, red pot on her way in; she was eager to get inside – if this picturesque garden was any indication of what was inside, of what was yet to come, then she would have it made! She would be in heaven, seventh heaven!

Maizey opened the matching red, front door. She stepped inside and immediately moved to one side.

Blue Bell hesitantly stepped through the open door, unsure of what to expect. People can say a lot of things, but you don't always know whether it's true or not, the thought did flash through her busy mind.

Even so, she entered the unknown hallway with Maizey by her side. Blue Bell was pleasantly surprised...

The first thing she noticed, was sweet smelling flowers everywhere. It was like the garden simply continued into the charming home. Maizey really loved flowers *and* she really had a way with flowers, with plants it would seem.

A smile formed on her young face, Blue Bell felt luckier and luckier, by the second. She noticed the quality of light inside, it appeared different, it somehow seemed alive... "Do you like it?" Maizey interrupted her train of thought.

"It seems nice," Blue Bell answered slightly dry. She did not want to give away how and what she really felt. If Maizey knew her true motive, then she would be out of here in a flash. Considering everything, she did not want to hurt Maizey (or anyone, for that matter!) nor her good intentions. Blue Bell definitely needed this woman's kindness and her home, her lovely home.

"Nice," Maizey repeated, "you could see it that way, but you'll miss out on a lot, looking at things like that." She took one step back as if she was giving the young one space. Also, she wanted this girl to see what is really in front of her.

Blue Bell looked at her nervously – what was this woman trying to do? She always thought that *she* was the strange one, but it would appear that she wasn't alone in this pool of weirdness. But in all fairness, Maizey might rather be seen as eccentric, and not really weird, Blue Bell conceded.

"Do you still think it's nice?" Maizey asked with veiled boldness as they entered the not-at-all boring living-room.

Silence, that was what Maizey got from Blue Bell. It took her a few moments, to take everything in... the sheer number of ornaments... and trinkets... and figurines. Blue Bell didn't know where to look. The whole room was filled with colourful ornaments of all shapes and sizes, even tiny figurines she never even knew existed.

Maizey still heard only silence from Blue Bell, not even a peep. The girl must be overwhelmed by the absolute volume of ornaments filling the tiny room – the older woman gave a smile; a wide, sweet smile. She could sense that this young girl was only holding up a facade, and if you 'poked' long enough, you would be able to poke enough holes so that the whole thing collapsed. Hmm, she contemplated, interesting. Was there a challenge here? Was she prepared to accept this challenge?

"Where did you get this?" Blue Bell finally said while holding up a pink glass bowl. It happened to be one of Maizey's favourites.

"That particular one I found in India. I remember it very well," Maizey made herself comfortable in her rocker as if this was going to be a long story, "it was in a tiny, crowded shop, which was more a shack than anything else."

Blue Bell followed her example and nestled in one of her easy chairs while holding the little glass bowl this way and that. She liked the way the light, the afternoon light, bounced off it. It made the pink appear even more pink.

"... in any case that was how I acquired that piece." Blue Bell only now realised that she wasn't paying attention – she only had eyes for the pink glass bowl resting in her delicate hands. "You really like it," Maizey noticed and this time Blue Bell heard.

"Yes, I quite like it. It looks so... oriental... go figure." She gave a little laugh as if she was hiding something.

Maizey still have not figured this one out. It would seem that there were many sides to this young girl. Uncovering just one, was a small victory in itself; imagine uncovering all of them...

"Are you hungry?" she asked already getting up. "Would you like to see the rest of the house?" she asked again before Blue Bell could answer. After a tiny pause, she indicated that she would love to see the rest of Maizey's lovely home.

Joe, still reeling from his revelation, almost forgot the time, he almost forgot about food and about dear old Pup. He was moving about clumsily, restlessly. Understandable, Joe thought, "Poor fella, you must be starving," he exclaimed loudly and made coddling sounds which got Pup really going. Joe picked him up, ever so gently, and raised him to eye-level, "You are some special something, aren't ye?" Again making his coddling sounds.

Casey loved the attention – now that 'Blue-girl' was gone, it was up to Joe to give him any and all attention. Luckily, Joe liked doing it; having Pup around sure made life much more pleasant, and on top of that, it did something for Joe. He could feel it in his heart, although he wouldn't admit it aloud, it sure did do something to his heart. Maybe it was softening him, but for what, Joe wondered.

He remembered seeing a diner nearby and decided to head on over with Pup safely hidden in his oversized brown jacket. In his pocket, he could feel the pink key-ring pressing against his thigh. Again, it reminded him of Blue Bell. Was she okay, he asked himself this nagging question and the other nagging one: where was she?

Her cell phone has been quiet for some time now, and he still could not decipher the initials 'JC'. The best he could come up with was 'Casey'; he did not know what the 'J' was for. He knew it was her brother, but the 'J' threw him. "Brother Casey..." He shook his head discouragedly, yet firmly.

This whole 'Blue-girl'-business was wearing him down; just one more reason to do what *he* had set out to do, and come hell or high water, he – Joe Mountain – would see this through!

It started to rain and Joe quickened his pace. He could see the diner, its glow was like a beacon in the sudden downpour. He reached the glass door just in time, before he was completely soaked. He shook off most of the droplets and again headed for the end-most booth.

Once seated, and resting his limbs from the sudden exertion (he wasn't a young man anymore!), he could at last take in his surroundings. Joe must admit: it wasn't a bad-looking eating joint. It was actually quite good, pleasant even...

"What would you like?" a man's voice interrupted his transitory scrutiny. The tall thin man laid out their menus in front of Joe. "These are our specials," he pointed with long fingers toward a single leaflet, "do you see anything you like?"

This young man had a quick pace about him which Joe did not like, at all! You shouldn't rush Joe Mountain...

"Did I mention our specials...?"

"Yes, you did," Joe stopped him in his tracks. His voice had a certain authority, a certain strength, that wasn't there before. Joe was stunned for a moment or two, before he quickly resumed is reply; he didn't want to give 'Snapper' a gap.

He placed his order patiently and deliberately – you don't rush Joe. He made sure that there would be warm milk for Pup *and* some veggies. Joe believed that he should eat the same as Joe – no dog food for this little guy!

A yapping waiter finally stormed off to his next table, leaving Joe with a big grin. It was nice winning for a change, he thought as he cradled Casey next to him on the roomy seat. The little fella was wide awake, paying full attention – ye know, food was involved. And Joe noticed that he was paying more and more attention to Joe *and* his words.

It made him feel, so good. That he actually meant something to someone, even if it was just a dog, and what a cute one it was.

Joe described the diner to him, pointing unobtrusively. Pup listened eagerly, he even listened closely to Joe tattling about 'Snapper', their funny-looking waiter. He did notice his jewellery which he wore on his face and his black tattoo which he proudly showed off on the side of his thin long neck... nonetheless, Joe had his suspicions.

When 'Snapper' briefly returned with his black coffee, and opened his mouth to announce the "ETA" of his food, he squarely confirmed Joe's suspicions; 'Snapper' was indeed gay, a tutti-frutti. A few things became clear now... a few things made sense now...

"...ketchup with your food?" the young gay waiter dispersed Joe's thoughts for a moment.

"Aye, ketchup would be good. Remember my extra portion of 'veggie-mix'," Joe kindly reminded 'Snapper'. Before he could blink, 'Snapper' was on his way again, off to another crowded table. Hmm, Joe only now noticed how noisy it was, all the clamouring voices mixed together in this confined space... It made him a bit uneasy... He felt a wet nose poking at his large folded hand. Pup reminded him of his presence and Joe immediately calmed down, till his breathing was normal again.

'Snapper' soon arrived with his steaming plate of food. Joe's mouth started watering as he inhaled all the aromas. His green eyes darted all over his heaped up plate of food. He did manage a "thank you" though, before he sank his white teeth into his first bite, and what a heavenly bite it was!

He remembered the wee fella, and stole small pieces of food from his plate and fed them patiently, very carefully to his loyal companion. The generous helpings on his large white plate impressed Joe immensely – he had a healthy appetite, and appreciated anyone who cared enough, to notice.

Maybe, 'Snapper' wasn't such a dodgy character after all. Maybe, he was okay underneath all that tutti-frutti weirdness. Joe chuckled softly – sometimes he could be such a stook, such a muppet, such a spanner... take your pick. That's Joe.

CHAPTER ELEVEN

Blue Bell woke up early. At first, she didn't know where she was. She felt completely out of place, out of whack. But then, slowly, it dawned on her: she was in her own room in Maizey Mountain's lovely home!

Maizey! It all started coming back; the mark, the magical garden, the house filled with every ornament you can imagine. Oh yeah, she was wide awake now!

She felt slightly embarrassed for thinking of Maizey as a mark. Poor woman, she deserved better!

She was no mark; she was a good-hearted, caring individual, who happened to love ornaments. It would seem that it was rather about decorating (decorating the garden, decorating her home, and even decorating herself!), than merely collecting all these beautiful things.

After making her bed – she felt she had to – she stood in the middle of her cosy room, looking at her all black outfit.

For the first time in her life, Blue Bell did not feel like putting on her black armour, because that was exactly what it was: her armour. It kept her hidden *and* it kept her safe. Safe from all the hurt out there. The rejection. The disapprovals. The judgements. *All* of it.

Why on earth, did she feel this way, today, right here, right now, she asked herself with a perplexed look on her delicate face. Her bright blue hair stood unruly which only added to her deeply confused facial expression.

Blue Bell still stood wondering about her clothing when she heard the unexpected knock on her bedroom door. After a slight pause, she opened the wooden door slowly, only to find a sleepy Maizey still dressed in her nightgown.

"Can I help you?" It slipped out before Blue Bell could even try to stop it. Being this way – so mouthy – was so natural to her, she sometimes forgot, but she won't forget again! She will make sure of that – she bit her tongue, maybe too hard, but it worked!

"Good morning, Maizey," she tried again, softening her voice and her demeanour as she spoke, "can I help you?"

"Morning Blue Bell," Maizey returned her polite greeting. "When I woke up, I suddenly realised that you might need fresh clothes." She stepped closer, trying to spy, quickly, what if any clothing she had. She tried to remember Blue Bell's backpack – what did it look like? All she remembered, was that it was teeny tiny...

"Unfortunately," Blue Bell took a deliberate pause, "all I have, is this." She pointed towards the jet black outfit draped across the beige wingback-chair in her medium-sized room. She looked back at Maizey with what she hoped was an angelic face, blue hair and all.

"Come with me!" Maizey ordered and marched Blue

Bell to *another* bedroom.

Although the room was empty of people, it looked like someone lived or had lived there once upon a time. The look was dated, even the posters against the walls; it was of stars, long forgotten. This puzzled Blue Bell, but she didn't show any of her feelings. She just walked in, naturally, pretending that it, everything was normal.

Maizey opened the cupboard's louvered doors one by one, exposing clothing of different sizes and colours. She started flipping through them while muttering indistinctive words.

Blue Bell slowly twirled around, checking everything out. It was so eerie – it seemed and felt like this particular room was trapped somewhere in the '80s. Blue bell was stunned; the curtains with colourful large print, the frilly bedding, the block-patterned carpets, even the bedside lamp... it was shaped like a dolphin...

"What about this?" Maizey finally got her attention. She held up a purple top with a neon-pink hart in the centre. Blue Bell pulled a face, and Maizey immediately bundled it back in the overfilled maroon cupboard.

Next up, a yellow shirt with tiny red dots. Blue Bell could hardly look at it, it made her blue eyes hurt. Maizey just smiled and again, returned the unwanted garment. Her chubby hand reached for a bright blue t-shirt, and Blue Bell instinctively knew: that's the one. She smiled as Maizey held up the blue t-shirt. Blue Bell straight away grabbed it and held it tightly against her chest.

"I'm guessing you like it," Maizey teased and started looking for matching pants, or maybe she would prefer a pair of shorts. When she turned around again, Blue Bell already had on the bright blue t-shirt. "It matches your hair," she observed laughingly while she placed a pair of white shorts and a pink denim on the three-quarter bed.

Blue Bell inspected each, and after a very short deliberation, picked the pink denim. "Would you mind?" she asked self-consciously, looking down.

"No, no," Maizey replied hastily, waving her chubby hands before her. "Take your time," she ordered and closed the door mindfully behind her.

Alone! At last! Was it appropriate to think it, to feel it? Very relieved? Blue Bell just shook it off, and started climbing into the slightly tight, pink denim. It was a soft pink, which balanced the brightness of her t-shirt. Otherwise she would be walking around like a bright billboard, advertising a nursery school or something!

Blue Bell decided to look through the rest of the built-in cupboard, seeing how she was alone and everything. She couldn't believe the amount of clothing she saw... There must be like fifty or sixty different outfits, and the funny thing was, it was clothing in different sizes, from children's wear up to adult wear... What was going on here?

Oh my God!

"Even the shoes!" she exclaimed as she lightly stroked each pair. She heard an unexpected sound and immediately closed the maroon doors. She quickly grabbed her own clothing and left in a hurry. The sound she had heard, turned out to be Maizey vacuuming.

"How odd," Blue Bell whispered as she climbed down the wooden stairs. "Vacuuming this early?"

Maizey switched off the machine as soon as she saw Blue Bell.

"Would you like some coffee?" she offered while

wiping her forehead. Cleaning was hard work, especially at her age.

"Yes, but," Blue Bell answered uncertain, "aren't you having any?"

"You know, getting an early start, is always a good thing. Especially in a house this big," she smiled as she gestured at the space around her.

Blue Bell lingered slightly before she responded. "I, I will give you a hand, if you like," she volunteered hesitantly, not sure what to expect.

"If I like! If I like!" Maizey exclaimed loudly. Blue Bell contracted a little and then immediately relaxed as Maizey continued. "My dear child, getting help, any help, at my age, is a huge bonus. Managing this home alone can be challenging. Managing both my flower shop and my home is a definite tight-rope." She took a breath and almost looked tired. She handed Blue Bell her coffee in a very decorative mug, while helping herself to a second cup.

They both sat down at the kitchen table which reminded the young girl of sunflowers and farms and... happiness. She frowned deeply while looking deep into her mug. Happiness, she thought again. What was that again?

She felt completely shocked that she felt this way! And thought this way! Luckily, Maizey asked about breakfast, and Blue Bell could once again, forget about truths like this. Ugh! Truths!

"I would like toast, just plain toast," she answered hastily, before her troubling thoughts could run away with her to some dark place, which she desperately tried to avoid – sometimes at all cost!

"Toast, just plain toast?" Maizey asked rhetorically with complete incredulity, "I think not! You will have a proper meal with me. Remember, cleaning is a lot of work, *and* it's going to be a long day!"

The older woman looked at Blue Bell intently, almost as if she was trying very hard to get a closer look inside her head, her blue head. Blue Bell's defences immediately shot up. Her 'inside', her head-space was very private to her *and* it was her head-space. The only one she ever allowed, was her beloved brother... Okay, okay, maybe even 'Cave-man', but that was a long time ago...

"Right!" Maizey slapped her meaty thighs and got up. "Tell you what, I'll make us some scrambled eggs *and* toast, but it won't be plain. How's that?" she asked intimidatingly, but before Blue Bell could open her mouth to speak, she just rattled on.

Blue Bell thought it best to keep quiet. Maizey was a strong woman, maybe a bit old, but by no means done for. She can also be a bit overbearing; besides, it was her home after all and Blue Bell was a mere guest in it.

In the end, Blue Bell was talked (more like bullied) into a healthy portion of scrambled eggs and toast, which was decorated with fried onions and tomatoes.

So, no plain toast... but she must admit: it was damn good!

Later that day, while standing in the familiar flower shop, Blue Bell fully realized the importance of her hearty breakfast, and of Maizey's words. She has been standing at the counter, holding a finicky stick, now for hours. It wasn't really a stick, it was an elaborate branch of something and it felt like Maizey was taking forever to get it right.

Blue Bell had to move it this way and that, but each

time the fastidious shop owner just wasn't satisfied. Or was she just being thorough? Either way, the young teen was getting irritable. And irritability wasn't something she could afford just yet. It most definitely would trigger other unpleasant and uncalled-for emotions that Blue Bell would much rather avoid. Not only are they extremely bothersome and hard, having them would or could jeopardize her stay – her staying, was at the top of her list, for now, anyway.

"Maizey, how long have you been here?" she asked in an effort to take her mind off her emotional state. Roller-coasting emotions had to be banned for now.

"Oo, let me see now," Maizey started answering her question, "it was probably..." It was working. All she had to do now was to listen with *both* ears, and her rocking emotions would soon be forgotten. "...yes, that is quite a long time, wouldn't you say?"

She took a breath and with the green garden shears still in her fleshy hand, she brushed some of her greying hair away from her forehead. Maizey was actually not bad-looking. Blue Bell could see that perhaps a long time ago, she would have been quite a catch.

She blushed a little, and looked away. Even on her tanned face, you would be able to see.

"It's hard work, isn't it?" Maizey prompted some more for a reaction, for her participation. "Everyone thinks that arranging flowers, selling flowers, giving advice on flowers, is but lickedy-pickedy-lickedy-poop, no biggy."

Blue Bell let go of the fancy branch as she burst out laughing, little giggles at first, which steadily flowed into more free, relaxed laughter. Even Maizey, joined in the fun. It turned out that she had a real nice, infectious laughter.

After about a minute or so, they both just looked at each other, breathing heavily after all that necessary laughter. Blue, young eyes were met by older, wiser translucent grey eyes. During that moment, something clicked for both women. Maybe differently for each, but something definitely clicked.

CHAPTER TWELVE

Dear Joe had slept late that morning. It was rather unusual for him, but even so, he slept late *and* he enjoyed it. The trick now, was to not feel guilty – Joe still had trouble with that one. At his very mature age, you would think that guilt was a thing of the past, not so.

You don't learn to just live with it. No, sir. You had to deal with guilt even more so as your age increased. And coupled with his 'colourful' past, it became an impossible task.

Having no booze also made it hard, extremely hard, because now, he wasn't able to forget. Whatever memories he had and could be unblurred, he had to face, without his liquor and by himself, on his own...

Joe immediately collapsed his strong arms beneath him and lay back down on the double bed. Why get up? He sighed forcefully. Why get up? Why? He kept asking himself, until he felt a familiar, tiny nose pressing up against his shoulder. He smiled automatically.

He turned his curly head and watched amused as Pup tried to climb on his hairy chest. He reached out and gently moved him closer. He was looking Pup squarely in his brown eyes and then greeted him very animatedly; telling him what a good boy he was... "yes he is." Joe got completely carried away by it, and soon forgot about his troubles.

Whistling. Joe got up whistling! What a turn-around! Maybe, just maybe, the day that Joe has been waiting for, for so long, has finally – at long last – arrived!

He remembered about the passage he had read in the Holy Bible as his muted green eyes glanced over the big black book with the embossed golden letters.

That much celebrated verse had set things in motion for Joe Mountain. The specific verse played itself before his eyes, 'I saw a dream which made me afraid, and the thoughts upon my bed and the visions of my head troubled me.' He once again realized the message in it and felt and understood the urge welling up inside of him.

He knew that to ignore this specific urge, would be bad for him and for his entire life. It was giving him a chance to rectify his mistakes, to unburden himself, *and* to be rid of his troubling visions (memories) and the accompanying fear. Be rid of it, permanently.

With this in mind Joe collected his keys, his wallet and Pup. He locked the door and caringly placed the 'pink' key in his pocket, once more. He gave strong, measured steps toward his favourite, blue-and-silver truck.

Once inside, he pushed Nancy into life. Safely buckled in, he checked on Pup, quickly, and shifted into first, into what he knew would be the rest of his life.

Joe knew exactly what his life has been like up until now. He was, in fact, not at all sure of what it would be like further down the road. How would the rest of his life progress, he wondered nervously, but even so continued on his new journey. He wasn't going to let anything or anyone deter him from his mission.

That was how it felt to him, like a mission. Not like a James Bond-mission, rather a Joe-mission. One he desperately wanted to complete, successfully. This time, he will!

He switched on the radio to calm his nerves; he was getting close now. Not only could he see it, but he could feel it, way down. This made him a bit nervous, maybe even a lot, but even so, he kept going. Closer and closer to his much feared destination, down the tarred road, closer and closer.

Joe exhaled loudly. Even Pup moved about restlessly, as if he could feel Joe's angst. He whimpered a bit. Joe reached over and stroked his tiny ears in an effort to calm him. He didn't want the wee fella to feel what he, Joe, felt.

It seemed to help. Pup quieted down and started watching the road interestedly, same as Joe.

Once again, Joe took in the very familiar surroundings, places he once knew, people he once knew. The road he was travelling on, seemed very familiar. When he entered his old neighbourhood, it too felt familiar. Even the house he used to live in, seemed familiar, especially the big red pot, seemed very familiar...

What was that? Were his eyes playing tricks on him,

or did he really just see what he thought he saw?

Joe went past slowly in an effort to try and sense whether this was good timing; was it a good idea to come now? As soon as he saw that unmistakable blue hair, he just passed the familiar house as fast as he could, hoping that no one saw, especially that Blue one.

What the hell was going on? He asked himself in total disbelief. He parked Nancy at the nearest filling station – there was no way he could continue. Not only his near impossible mission, but also driving. Joe was so shook up, there was no way in hell that he could continue driving; not even one more mile!

What the hell was she, 'Blue-girl', doing there? At that house? At his house?

Joe was deeply disturbed and completely unnerved by what he saw; rather, by WHO he saw. His whole body was shaking lightly, even his dull, green eyes couldn't or wouldn't focus properly...

Poor Casey didn't know what to do. He just lay quiet as a mouse, looking up at Joe with his little brown eyes; they looked worried. The little frown on his forehead just emphasized his worried look.

Joe was in such a state, he didn't even notice. His eyes didn't register anything. All the stormy activity was happening inside of him. All the anxious turmoil, coming and crashing through him, through his whole, aged body. His body may be big, but it still felt every shock, every wave, every crash, everything...

Blue Bell did hear the truck pass, but she wasn't

paying any attention. Maizey had shown her these spectacular white flowers. Tiny white flowers which were shaped like tiny, little bells. They were all bunched together hanging from springy deep-green, leafy branches.

What made them spectacular, wasn't how they looked – their shape or size – but what happened to them during night-time. They changed colour, going from their pure white raiment during the day to the most exquisite red at night... "Wow!"

Double wow, this time, silently. How on earth was this possible? How can a flower change its colour just like that? How? All these questions flashed through her brain, one by one.

Blue Bell was in awe; complete, gum-dropping awe. How on earth was such a thing even possible, she asked again.

The only answer her primordial brain could come up with, it is God's doing. It's a miracle, in a flower – who knew?

"They're lovely, aren't they?" the familiar voice asked as it came closer. It was Maizey.

"I didn't see you back there," Blue Bell replied slightly surprised, "yes, they are." She stood upright, still smelling the dainty flowers' dainty aroma – it was the sweetest, most gentle scent she had ever experienced.

"You have a lovely garden, Maizey. One could get lost in it."

Maizey looked at her appreciatively. Blue Bell could see her chest, her whole demeanour swelling with pride. "It truly is magnificent," her own eyes shone brightly with some sort of bliss; for how long, she did not know, but that they did, was all that mattered.

They spent the rest of the afternoon looking at each flower, at each plant, at each decorative piece throughout the whole yard. Blue Bell enjoyed it (to her own surprise!) tremendously. She enjoyed being surrounded by such beauty and green tranquility. The atmosphere was absolutely intoxicating. How Maizey had managed it all, and still managed it, was beyond her.

Satisfied that Blue Bell has seen every corner of the dazzling beauty, the two women, young and old, moved to the porch. There, they each sat comfortably, cushioned against the hard cane, in two big cane chairs. Between them stood a round cane table with a clear glass-top. A big glass jug, filled with freshly made lemonade, and two tall glasses were the only items decorating the small table. Except, of course, for the two round coasters sitting quietly beneath their glasses.

Blue Bell was busy studying her cork coaster. On one side you could see the bare cork, and on the other, you could get lost in a colourful display of the rainbow – every colour was as intense as the one before it...

"Was your hair always blue?" Maizey asked suddenly, tongue-in-cheek.

Blue Bell stared at her, gaping like a fish. She was stunned for a moment. She didn't know what to...

"I'm kidding!" Maizey exclaimed loudly, exaggerating with her fleshy arms. She burst out laughing – she couldn't help herself. Ha-ha-ha all the way, tears streaming down her cheeks.

When she finally got to her senses and regained control, she could manage a "you should have seen your face," before her contagious laughter took hold of her, again.

This time, it wasn't solo. A man's voice, joined in the fun...

CHAPTER THIRTEEN

It was late in the afternoon. The sun was beginning to set, turning everything into a fiery red, even the man, the older man, before her.

Maizey could not stop staring; all laughter seized, forgotten. She could not believe her eyes, she could not!

It was as if all her mental activity had frozen, had stopped completely. There simply wasn't anything, anything...

Even mouthy Blue Bell remained speechless; she was stunned, completely and utterly stunned. This man was the very last man she had expected here, in fact, she did not even expect him at all. And yet, here he stood, looming over them, shrouded in a bright red glow.

"A... ah... uh..." that was all Maizey could get out; uttering only nonsensical poppycock.

"What, what are you doing here?" Blue Bell finally came to Maizey's rescue nesciently. Her forwardness slowly, slowly came to the surface.

The man just looked at her briefly; his attention was leaning more towards the older woman. This baffled Blue Bell and raised questions faster than she could answer them. Joe was acting very, very strangely. She knew he was strange and unique to begin with, but this, this she could not comprehend. What was Joe doing here? How on earth did he find her? But more importantly, why was he acting so weird?

"Joe..." Maizey spoke for the very first time. She sat motionless. Only her lips moved when she uttered his name. Even her glassy grey eyes stood still in their sockets, completely transfixed on Joe's face. His incomprehensible face, glowing red in the late afternoon sun.

Blue Bell stepped closer, feeling inexplicably protective of her. Joe's weird behaviour, his impending silence, was making her nervous. "Joe, what are you doing here?" she dared asking nervously. "How did you find me?" She looked at him, her blue eyes even brighter and bigger than usual. Even the reddish incandescence, could not alter her blue-blue eyes.

Without warning Joe's stomach moved, showing tiny bumps. Blue Bell jumped back almost on top of her cane chair. Maizey looked alarmed at the frightened young girl. This somehow prompted her to get up, to get moving.

His stomach moved again; this time it was making funny noises. Maizey stared in disbelief at Joe's mid-section, not sure what to think, let alone what to expect.

Joe stepped back slowly as Blue Bell started giggling. His temporary shell-shock was beginning to wear off. Blue Bell giggled even louder, relaxing completely into her cushioned chair.

Maizey was looking back and forth as though she attended a tennis match. One was busy splitting her sides with laughter, the other was beginning to come around with his moving, talking tummy...

"Lickedy-pickedy-lickedy-poop. What the hell is going on here?"

She looked in Joe's direction with her hands held up. "Joe, Joe. What are you doing here?" She moved around precariously on the wide porch. Blue Bell tugged at her fleshy arm and prompted her to sit down, "calm down," she added, her voice still filled with laughter.

Maizey looked at the young one, confusion written all over her experienced face.

"Joe is not strapping or hiding a weapon, or anything like that," Blue Bell came to Joe's rescue this time, as she explained calmly. Joe came closer, real slow at first, but then more confidently as Blue Bell told Maizey everything. Everything about her first encounter with Joe – the 'Cave-man' (this made Maizey smile and made her relax a little); their journey 'home' (it was actually his home; hers was still undecided); even about how she had come across Maizey's path.

"And that moving bump," she pointed towards Joe's stomach, who was waiting patiently by the famous big red pot, "that's only little Casey." Maizey looked even more confused and frowned as Blue Bell held out her thin arms.

Joe complied. He carefully revealed a tiny white pup wearing a brown mask, and placed him ever so gently in Blue Bell's awaiting arms.

A quiet Maizey just stared in amazement at the whole picture unfolding before her relaxed eyes and ears. "So, you two know each other..." It was more an observation rather than a question. She seemed lost once more; current events had not fully sunk in yet. So she simply stared into space, trying subconsciously to avoid the low hanging sun – he will surely flash you every chance he gets.

Blue Bell cuddled little Casey and wasn't paying any attention. Right now, it seemed the best course of action for her. It was obvious that these two also knew each other; she just didn't know how. Maybe she would get a chance of finding that missing puzzle piece, and then a whole lot of mystery, especially about Joe, would make sense.

"Maizey. Maizey, can, can, can we talk," Joe stammered and almost faltered, but carried on, even so. "Privately," he added while peering quickly in Blue Bell's direction. He cleared his throat softly to emphasize his words and his intention.

Blue Bell did not need any encouragement to leave. She quietly stood up with Casey safely in her arms and disappeared as quietly into the empty house.

"Maizey," Joe tried again, still standing by the big red pot. His long legs felt weak, but he hid it as best he could. His age didn't help any, but what the hell? For him, it was now or never; he could feel it in his gut. If he did not go through with this – his mission – he, Joe Mountain, would die an old sad man, *and* a lonely regretful man...

Maizey refused to look at him. Her eyes would only look at the open space around him.

"Maizey," he tried once more with more feeling in his mature voice.

"Excuse me," she said abruptly and stood up, still

avoiding his searching green eyes. "Sit. I'm going to fetch you a glass." Maizey left him standing there by the familiar flower pot.

Joe hesitated for a moment or two, and then slowly and quietly took a seat, awaiting his dreaded 'trial'. He stared at the beautiful garden, not really looking at anything specific, when something caught his eye. It looked like it could be a smallish wheel.

He decided to investigate and walked the few steps with more ease. The smallish wheel was sticking out from beneath a cascading fern.

Joe pushed the leaves aside, and saw that the wheel was actually attached to something. He pulled on it. Nothing. He pulled on it some more.

Finally the object was free... and Joe was in tears...

Blue Bell came out the charming house, holding one glass in her delicate hand. She was looking for Joe when she finally spotted him in the garden. He was kneeling on the soft green grass. He was looking intently at something, but she couldn't be sure what. When she almost reached him, she heard funny noises escaping his mouth.

It took her a moment to realize – dummy! – that the man, 'Cave-man', was crying, he was busy crying!

She came to a complete halt. She almost retreated, like backing off all the way... but then, something blocked her urge to just run...

Instead, Blue Bell just watched Joe, this giant-like man, sitting, shaking, crying. What was she to do? She didn't feel confident enough to help, to console him. Not only wasn't she good at that sort of thing, she also did not know Joe well enough and long enough to say (hopefully) the right words.

Where's Maizey? She wondered. That woman was more suited for this type of situation, and apparently, the two of them, knew each other.

Maizey merely pressed a clean glass in her hand and told her to take the glass to Joe; he was sitting outside.

Blue Bell took a shaky step forward, closed her eyes, and took another. Her hand instinctively reached out and gently touched Joe's broad shoulders. Her own hand was shaking so bad, she had difficulty just holding it there.

For a brief moment, the crying stopped, but then, it started again, like raw unmollified sobs tearing through his whole colossal body, even worse than before.

She pulled back her hand like a bee had stung her and remained frozen like a statue. Never in all her life, has she ever seen a man – a Goliath – cry like that!

She never thought that she would ever... and yet, here he was, crying his heart out, like it was the end of the world. What could be so bad, she wondered as she unfroze slightly. What?

And where was Maizey? She asked again very irritated. She knew full well that she had ups and downs, but this, this was too much. She was beginning to get annoyed with this whole scenario, and decided to retreat little by little.

She had just started to move back, when she heard his voice. "Blue Bell. Blue Bell." He was calling her name. His voice was soaked with sadness, obviously, but also something else... maybe... guilt?

She couldn't be sure (she was no expert), but in any case, she could not leave now! She could not leave HIM now!

Blue Bell kneeled beside Joe, feeling the softness and coolness of the deep-green grass. She felt very nervous, very unsure of herself. And unsure of what to expect.

He laid his huge hand on her petite knee. His green eyes were closed. It almost looked as if he was praying. She could also see the mystery object from before.

It was a miniature wheelbarrow. It was lying on its side and by the looks of it, it was rather old, and dirty, very dirty. Red, could have been its original colour – it was faded now and of course, it was dirty. So, it was hard to say...

"Blue Bell," Joe paused briefly and slowly opened his damp eyes, "where is Maizey?"

"She, she's still inside," Blue Bell answered hesitantly. She looked him carefully in the eye, ready to bolt, if necessary.

"Where is Pup?" he asked, just staring in front of him, his hand still resting on her itchy knee.

"He is also inside," she looked at him stiffly and quickly added, "with Maizey." She studied his ominous-looking face quickly and tried very hard to gauge exactly where he was at; still ready to bolt at a moment's notice.

"Can I talk to you?" he asked strangely, "I feel like talking."

"E, ur..." Before she could finish, he uttered more strange words, "I need to talk. Maizey won't listen, I know she won't."

Again, he paused briefly, and looked straight at her, "Will *you* listen?"

He sounded desperate. His whole face was pleading with every movable muscle. How could she say no?

And so, the story began, Joe's trial began...

CHAPTER FOURTEEN

It was a hot summer's day like any other. Joe and Maizey had just finished some much needed gardening. Everything looked hunky-dory once again. But that was where the hunky-dory part had stopped...

The couple sat on their happy porch enjoying the welcoming cool shade and their icy lemonade. He could still hear the ice-cubes jingle in his moist glass. Their daughter was playing on the freshly cut lawn, pushing her wee wheelbarrow, pretending to be a gardener.

Joe sat smiling very contently, taking a cool sip every so often. He remembered Maizey shouting instructions to their daughter and laughing each time she tipped her little red wheelbarrow. Everyone had fun. Everyone had a good time...

He broke down momentarily, wiping his puffy eyes with his usual red-and-white bandana. Blue Bell waited patiently, listening intently; she knew that this moment was crucial to Joe, to getting out whatever needed to get out. She knew full well, what happened if you did not get things out...

He returned once more to that fateful day. Blue Bell could see that it was extremely hard and painful for him. She gave his resting hand a gentle squeeze, trying to reassure him. He nodded gratefully and bravely continued his life-story.

He was still sitting complacently, his wife was still laughing, the sun was still shining, when all of a sudden, Maddie just collapsed, like fell to the ground like a sack of potatoes. She just lay there apparently unconscious; her small body was shaking violently.

Joe and Maizey had raced to her side. Joe got there first. He immediately fell to the ground trying to help, trying to wake her, trying to make the shaking stop. But that was all he did: try. They both did. Without any success...

Then, just as the shaking had started, it just stopped, completely. They both hovered over her small face, trying desperately to wake her.

All of a sudden, her blue eyes flew open and stared into space. Not looking at Joe, not looking at Maizey – just space.

Joe and Maizey looked at each other with *deep* concern. Joe felt deeply worried. He could still feel that, those anxious moments he had experienced; his wife's face – her alarmed face.

Joe remembered picking up Maddie; her tiny body limp in his arms; his wife freaking out, running to call an ambulance, a doctor, something...

In the end, they took her to hospital. He was driving like a crazy person; his wife was crying while stroking the still child's long hair.

He told Blue Bell about her still, blue eyes; how extremely eerie that felt. This was not the child he remembered, the child who was running around with her red wheelbarrow, just a moment ago!

Again, he had to take a break. It was harder than he anticipated; seeing everything again, hearing everything again, *feeling* everything again.

Aye! Indeed it was – HARD!

After many tests, many hours, many agonizing moments, the 'clever' doctors had come up with nada, nothing, diddly squat!

Joe could not believe his ears. How on earth was that possible? He had asked himself and Maizey and the 'clever' doctors a million times! How? He pleaded, Maizey pleaded, he begged, he threatened, he sobbed, but in the end, he was defeated, hopeless and mad as hell!

Blue Bell could see all those volatile emotions running through his incited green eyes.

"*That* was probably the hardest thing I ever had to deal with," he sighed deeply, some more emotions ran through him; leaving their mark, once again, whether he liked it or not.

"We thought that by some miracle or with more luck or even, with more time, Maddie would recover. Sadly, she did not... We, *I* had to face the ugly, ugly truth: my child was going to die, and there wasn't a damn thing *I* could do about it! Not a damn thing!"

Blue Bell, feeling more at ease now, moved closer and folded her thin arm beneath his muscular arm. "I don't know about you, but I can't hold this position much longer..." she said softly in an effort to get him to the porch, but also to lighten the tense mood, even for just a moment.

Joe slowly stood up, stretching his long limbs as he did so. "Ogh, time isn't always kind, is it?" he asked more rhetorically than anything else. He left the painful red wheelbarrow and aimed for the porch, hoping for some release, maybe some new perspective.

Blue Bell walked quietly beside him; she was getting to know this memorable porch, very well.

Both got seated, one quietly and one with a big sigh – the story wasn't finished yet. Joe's hardship, had only just begun...

After a very long and torturous journey, Joe and Maizey had lost their sweet, young Maddie. They were now completely childless (what a horrible thought!) and bloody heaven gained one more. Joe clenched his teeth; the mere thought, the mere memory of it all, made him feel bitter all over again. He could literally taste the aged bitterness in his mouth.

"I can't even begin to imagine what..."

"Spare yourself. Don't imagine it. Don't have children," he interrupted her grievously. She has never seen a face look so aggrieved, so resentful. She has never heard a voice so filled with pain... "Do ye not agree?" he interrupted again.

This was a new Joe, one she was not familiar with, not at all!

But even so, puzzle-pieces were being collected rapidly, although unpleasantly, they were definitely being collected, and soon she would have the whole picture.

"After that, things just fell apart." He stopped briefly as if reliving something, and then continued with a heavy heart.

Blue Bell leaned forward in an attempt to hear every word. His bitter anger muffled some of his words and mingled with his slight Irish accent, she really had to prick her two ears in order to catch every painful and difficult word.

"I turned to liquor, Maizey turned to God first and then to her own fantasy-land. That was where I lost her, and eventually she lost me. And that was that!"

Again, he lost himself in his painful, fuzzy memories...

Eager as she was, Blue Bell wished that Maizey would come. This really was her department, *and* Joe was her husband, after all!

"My trips became longer and longer, and eventually, I just stopped coming home. It wasn't easy, but what else could I do?" Another rhetorical question.

Blue Bell thought that *her* life was bad, a complete mess. But this, this just simply takes the cake! She can't even begin to imagine what that was like for Joe and for Maizey! The suffering, losing a child, the years and years of suffering since then... Oh my God, she thought loudly in her blue head.

Apparently his wife, Maizey, refused to let go and accept their daughter's premature and sudden death. Joe just looked deeper and harder into the bottle. It almost destroyed him, but lucky for him, he was strong enough to overcome his own, personal meltdown. Having a few, good friends also didn't hurt...

"Why did you decide to come back? Now?" Blue Bell dared asking some tough questions. Living here, meant caring about what happened to Maizey – it would directly affect her. And, Blue Bell had no intention of going home, so, she had to make this work.

Hopefully, Joe would not make too many waves. She

realized that this was extremely hard on everyone, but seriously she had herself to worry about. Nobody else will!

"It's actually quite funny. I was reading the Bible, the Holy Bible, and it landed me here. Now. I wasn't plannin' on actually coming, but things happened, necessary things. I suppose my time is now, to set things right, to make amends, to finish what I had started."

He looked at her with real determination, determination she had not seen before. Maybe, just maybe, Joe would be able to set things right. Aside from the obvious, it would benefit her greatly, because then she would have what she could call 'home'.

Fingers crossed...

She would support Joe any which way she could, hundred percent Blue Bell support. She would be his greatest aficionado; his very own, personal 'cheerleader'...

"Do you think I can do that?" he asked all of a sudden. "Do you think Maizey would talk to me? Hear me out?" His voice was so sincere *and* vulnerable, yes vulnerable, that was what she saw in his weary eyes.

She felt sorry for him. Poor Joe.

She crossed her legs and looked up. "I will do whatever I can to help, Joe. Maizey is one fine lady with depth. It really surprised me – her hidden depth." She reached over and gave him an encouraging pat on his enormous hand.

"If I were you, I would fix this, most definitely. It's obvious you care a great deal for her, and I would not let her get away, a second time." She studied his exhausted face carefully. She knew that doing what he did, and still wanted to do, took guts. Some serious guts.

"I'm pretty sure that she would at least listen. Maybe not the way you intend, but she'll hear you out! I know she will."

Joe wasn't convinced. He knew exactly what he had done many, many years ago... and if she didn't want to give him the time of day, he couldn't and wouldn't blame her. He remembered full well...

"You left me! Remember!"

How many times had he heard that? She was almost screaming her words, her face red with anger. They had this exact same argument many times before, and the funny thing was: she was right. Maizey was right.

Joe left, not because he wanted to, he left because she left him no choice. How can you relate to someone who doesn't want to live in the real world, who doesn't want to talk about things, who doesn't want to accept the truth: their daughter was dead and they could not do a damn thing about it, and (this one he kept to himself!) she chose to live, to stay in her fantasy-land – it made everything that much harder!

"Nothing to say? When faced with the truth, that is all you do, all you've ever done: run!"

What could he say? She was right again...

All of a sudden, the porch-light came on. Neither of them had noticed the early darkness which slowly enveloped the charming house. The red sun had made space for a silvery crescent moon.

Blue Bell saw it as a sign which only confirmed her proposal.

"Joe," she said full of feeling and made her proposal. "Why don't you come back tomorrow? You know, to give Maizey some time to deal with your unexpected," and even more softly, "and obviously troubling return." She took a breath. Her nerves were a bit frazzled, and thus, she hoped that dear Joe would accept her proposal. She really and truly did not feel like taking any more. It has been a *long* day...

"Maybe you're right." Here we go, she thought happily, blinking her blue eyes complacently. "Besides, I have come this far, haven't I?" He looked at her as if asking for her corroboration.

That was easy, "Yes, yes, you have. What you did took a lot of guts, Joe. A lot of guts."

He seemed pleased with her answer. "Where's Casey?" he finally asked as he got up. He never drank his lemonade. Suddenly sadness filled his green eyes as more memories came rushing back. This place, he thought, it still held some power over him. Even after all these long years, it did!

"I'll get him." She flew into the dimly lit house and reappeared after only a few seconds. "I'm gonna miss you," she said softly to Pup, and gave him a big kiss on his little forehead.

With Pup safely secured in his oversized brown jacket, he said his goodbyes and left.

Blue Bell wasn't completely sure whether she would see him the next day, but time would tell.

CHAPTER FIFTEEN

Blue Bell did not see Maizey, at all, that evening. On the one hand, she felt relieved (dealing with one spouse, was hard enough!), but on the other, she felt troubled by Maizey's reaction and hence, unsure of what tomorrow would bring. Her future was hanging in the balance...

Lucky for her, tomorrow had brought a happy, smiling Maizey making breakfast for two in her crowded kitchen. Blue Bell had to blink twice to make sure, she even rubbed her blue eyes a few times. There she was, making pancakes no less. And she began to hum. What the...

"Would you like some maple-syrup with your pancakes, Maddie?"

Maizey's words brought Blue Bell to a complete stop, like not even slowing down or reducing speed – NO – a complete and total stop. Even in her brain, everything stood still, completely still!

Maizey turned to look at her; her silence was taking too long. Maizey suddenly smiled widely and exclaimed in a high-pitched voice: "Oh my goodness! You're wearing the purple top I got you. Oh my goodness! Just look at you!" She held her chubby hands to her own face, "Even the little pink heart sits just right!"

Blue Bell, with her mobility slowly returning, backed up a few paces. Maizey was scaring her, she was actually scaring her! She backed up even more.

"Why don't you sit down?" Maizey gestured towards one of the chairs.

"Mama will make you a nice cup of tea." She turned back towards the gas stove, "It will most definitely sooth your nerves. You needn't worry. It's just a new school like any other, and you will make new friends in no time..."

Maizey was still talking when Blue Bell reached her room. Damn! She didn't have her cell with her. Damn!

She paced the whole length of the room, behind a closed door. If she could find the key, it would have been locked!

Her blue hair seemed bluer, almost electrifying. She must look like a mad woman, but she was freaking out here. No phone. No Joe. Joe!

Then it dawned on her, she would simply have to play along, until Joe came. "I hope to God, he does. God, I hope he comes!" she whispered audibly while looking around. What was she looking for?

She spun around, opened the door, and hurried to the dated room next door. It would be there. What? She wondered again. Then her stark blue eyes caught a glimpse of something and finally landed on what she was looking for.

There, in the corner, stood a stark white cane chair. It was flooded with toys, more specifically, dolls. One stood out. It was a peculiar-looking rag doll, and Blue Bell could tell that it must have been Maddie's favourite – it wasn't the cleanest, nor the newest. It actually looked quite worn, like the doll was played with, a lot!

She reached for it instinctively and held the quirky rag doll to her chest. It somehow made her feel better and gave her the necessary courage to do what she knew she had to do.

With 'Raggie' (her quick nick-name for the doll) safely, tightly tucked beneath her arm, she once again teedled-taddled to the unsure kitchen...

"Where have you been?" Maizey teasingly scolded her, "your pancakes are getting cold. I'll have to heat them up... and your tea..." she moved about feverishly, again with the humming.

Blue Bell took a seat; hopefully the right one.

Next moment, Maizey was on top of her loading off hot pancakes onto her empty plate. "Here you go, Sweetie." She almost hovered about like a clucking hen. It made Blue Bell feel uncomfortable, but she had to play along; hopefully not for long...

"Oh dear, I almost forgot about Tootsi." Again she hurried away getting a smaller plate, presumably for Tootsi, the rag doll.

Blue Bell shook her head; was this the same woman from yesterday, the one she had the pleasure of meeting and getting to know...

At last, Maizey came to rest, eating her own blueberry spangled pancakes.

"Do you want more syrup, Sweetie?" she asked sweetly, so caringly.

"No thanks, I'm good," Blue Bell answered warily, careful not to upset the pretence. "These pancakes are good," she complimented with her mouth full – anything to keep things calm, to keep things going, until...

"Don't speak with your mouth full. How many times..."

"Ok, ok. Sorry."

"That's better."

Blue Bell kept her mouth shut and swallowed every mouthful – although tasty – arduously. The sweet tea helped somewhat. She gave a quick glance towards Maizey; she seemed content, but even so, Blue Bell could not wish the seconds by, fast enough!

"Do you want to help Mama with the dishes?" Maizey asked abruptly.

"Sure," Blue Bell chose only one little word. Don't make waves, she reminded herself firmly, fervently.

She did not know how long this state would last, and she also wasn't familiar with it, thus she didn't know the intensity of Maizey's state. So, for now, she'll play it safe, until help arrived in the form of Joe.

Ding-dong!

The doorbell! Joe!

Ding-dong!

Blue Bell jerked her head up; her heart skipped a beat! Thank God! Joe!

She wanted desperately to rush to the front door, but kept herself in check with great difficulty.

Maizey stood up grumbling all the while, "We're busy having breakfast." She looked cross. Oh! Blue Bell thought. Please let it be Joe, please! She almost prayed.

Instead, she had to prick her young ears to hear who it was – please!

A woman's voice; it wasn't Joe. Damn!

"... just one cup, is all I need," she heard their voices coming this way.

An older woman appeared in the kitchen's doorway, curlers still in her grey hair. She was short, yet sturdy, and Blue Bell could have sworn that the busy-patterned coat she was wearing, was actually her dressing-gown!

"And who's this?" she immediately asked when she saw the blue-haired teen. She was ogling Blue Bell very overtly. "I don't think we've met..." She was still ogling, almost rudely now.

"Now, now Gladys! Where are your manners?" Maizey came to her rescue. She gave the other woman a stern look. She clicked her tongue and shook her head with her meaty hands resting firmly on her wide hips.

It did the trick, and Gladys turned her nosy nature towards Maizey. "Do you have a cup for me?" She was staring at the steaming teapot. She could not be more obvious. She was hoping for a quick cuppa while she had her daily gossip, of course.

"Oh, I'm afraid it's finished," Maizey replied with an innocent expression, "besides, it's not your kind." She hurried to get the sugar; filling her cup was top-priority.

They all stared at the pouring white crystals climbing to the top.

"All done!" Maizey remarked happily and gave Gladys her tea cup. Before she knew it, she was standing on the cold porch, saying a premature, reluctant goodbye.

"Thank heavens!" Maizey sighed loudly as she closed the door behind them. "Do you still want to help Mama with the dishes?" she asked ever so sweetly; she even smiled sweetly while she bent forward slightly.

Blue Bell quickly looked to and fro, before she answered meek and mild: "Yes Mama!"

Maizey was busy braiding Maddie's (Blue Bell's) hair. It was as if she hardly noticed the grown-up with the bright blue hair. This freaked Blue Bell out – how was this even possible? She knew from her own experience that things can go sideways, but this, this was a whole new ball-game!

Joe, where are you? She prayed silently. If Maizey didn't snap out of it, soon, what then? What will become of her? What will become of me, she asked worriedly.

"I love your hair," Maizey remarked pleased. She was in her element braiding her little girl's hair. She wanted her to look nice when they go out to her flower shop. She so enjoyed having her around; giving her little tasks to do...

Ding-dong!

The doorbell, again, louder this time!

"Gladys!" Maizey almost swore as she heard the second ding-dong. "That woman! She's enough to give anyone grey hair!" She stormed to the front door while Blue Bell stood watching wide eyed and wishing with all her might that she would see Joe's face, his angelic face...

Maizey opened the door forcefully, hastily and was about to snap at her nosy neighbour when she stopped mid-air, her mouth gaping like a fish in shock.

Blue Bell was too afraid to look, but did so anyway...
Joe! It was Joe! With his angelic face! Never in her
whole life, was she this glad to see someone, not just
anyone, but Joe!

She almost yelled out his name, but saw only then,
that he was not alone...

CHAPTER SIXTEEN

In his bulky arms he held Casey, and by his side stood a woman Blue Bell had not seen before. The thought flashed through her head: who was she and why was she here, with Joe?

Maizey unfroze and turned towards Blue Bell, "I want you to go upstairs, right now!" She said it slowly and clearly. It most definitely was an order.

Blue Bell turned to go, but before she could, Joe also gave an order of his own – his was more a favour than an order. He asked Blue Bell to take Casey with, but did so softly and caringly. She liked this Joe, especially Joe being *here*.

Now she would miss everything, the whole intense, painful and traumatic conversation. But she realised, nonetheless, that it was needed, seriously needed. Actually, if she were to be honest, she was glad and relieved that she could sit this one out.

Satisfied that Blue Bell was out of earshot, all three

adults got together in the crowded lounge. Maizey, Joe and the strange lady all sat down with definite spacing between them.

At first, there was only silence, a deafening silence all around them.

"Maizey," Joe broke the silence by going first. "Maizey, I know how you must feel..."

"You know nothing!" she said it with such intensity, it almost scared Joe. He wasn't used to this Maizey, or he had just forgotten, either way...

"How could you possibly know how I feel?" she asked looking straight at him, her plump cheeks began to discolour. "Where were you when I needed you the most?" she asked breathlessly, still looking at him with eyes filled with pain and bitterness and incredible turmoil.

Joe looked uncomfortably at the strange lady beside him, but she just nodded and nudged with her head for him to continue.

Bloody hell, he cursed inwardly. He wasn't sure if he could do this, after all. Was the Bible verse wrong, was his urge to come home wrong, was he wrong?

It felt as though his Joe-mission wasn't going so well, maybe it was all in vain and his mission was going to fail...

Stop complaining, and just get on with it! He reprimanded himself without any help.

"Where was I? Where was I?" he asked all worked up. "Let me tell you where."

"Easy Joe," the strange lady interjected and once again nodded for him to continue.

Joe had foolishly thought that she was on his side, and that she was here to back him. He frustratingly had to admit that this whole intercedence was actually for Maizey. He expected something like this – Maizey's apparent breakdown (regression) – and therefore brought a friend with, a very special friend...

Maizey knew her, but for some mysterious reason, she has forgotten her. Purposely or not, he couldn't be sure. Either way, she was here for Maizey, and help her, she would. Joe would too!

"When you became unreachable, I became drunk. And after a while of playing drunken fantasy-games, I had enough. I finally had enough. I was no shrink, so how on earth was I to help you?"

"You could have stayed," Maizey answered quickly. She seemed more relaxed now. Maybe there was hope, after all.

"No, I couldn't. I tried. Believe me, I tried. Nothing worked. Nothing helped, at least not my help..." He looked down, his green eyes suddenly felt tired, so tired. "The road became my sanctuary, my escape if you will. My truck became my home."

"As long as I stayed on the road, I knew I would be fine."

Maizey stared at him. Not with fury as before, but something else. Perhaps their rusty, dusty, broken-down love.

Joe did not see, but strange lady did. That was exactly what she was looking for. As long as there was love, there was hope, for both of them.

Joe called on her unexpectedly and arranged for her to meet at this familiar address. Familiar, yes, but so long ago... She was rather surprised to hear from him, and even more surprised to hear that his wife, Maizey, had regressed, yet again!

He mistakenly thought that she was here only for Maizey, but in actual fact, she was here for both of them. You cannot just fix one half of the problem; you have to fix both, in order to get the perfect solution. And that, was what she was hoping for, and aiming for – a perfect solution.

"Maizey, how do you feel about Joe, right now?" she asked tentatively.

"I'm, I'm not sure, Angela," Maizey answered in short and at the same time, a light-bulb-moment was born nesciently, just beneath the surface.

"How do you feel about yourself?" She knew this question was going to be hard, but it needed asking. Especially if they wanted to get to the bottom of things, and then to resolve this long dragging issue, once and for all!

"It depends," Maizey dared opening up which gave Angela all the ammo she needed. Now, she can help them, she can truly help them.

"Sometimes I'm sure of myself and my life, of where I'm going. Other times, I don't have a clue of who I am, of what I'm doing, of where I'll end up. Will it be on top, or..." She broke off abruptly and just stared off into the distance. "I have to check on Maddie," she excused herself and left in a big hurry.

Joe jumped up, but Angela waived him down and gestured with her eyes for him to stay put, be quiet.

"Angela, what the hell? How will we ever help her? Can she be helped?" the moment Maizey left, he spat out his words into the adorned living room.

"One step at a time, Joe, one step at a time," Angela soothed him with her pale two hands. "Don't you worry; just keep calm and let her speak. Let her get it all out, all the emotion, everything. Allow her to let go in her own way *and* most importantly on her schedule. Not yours!" Her voice was firm, yet gentle and caring.

Joe realised that she spoke the truth, and everything needed to be done a certain way, but even so, it was hard, bloody hard for him to just sit and hold back!

He too needed to say stuff, stuff which lay heavy on his mature heart!

It haunted him, it troubled him, and if he cared to admit it: it did take chunks, sizeable chunks, out of his life. And, as a matter of fact, he did desire to live out the remainder of his earthly days, without any regret, without any trouble, without... Actually, he just wanted peace!

Peace of mind. Peace in his heart. Peace in his ordinary Joe-life.

After what felt like ages, Maizey returned with a very confused-looking Blue Bell. Her whole face begged for an explanation, for an escape!

Joe had to contain his laughter. Besides the alarmed look on her young face, she had dear Casey in one hand, almost too tightly, and in the other she had that ugly doll! What was its name again?

He couldn't stop a smile escaping from his lips – a blue-haired teen, mouthy and all, stood before him while clutching a simple old rag doll...

"Maddie decided to join us," Maizey announced as she marched Blue Bell to the kitchen, "but first, time for some refreshments, wouldn't you say?" They both disappeared through the white swing-door.

"What now?" Joe asked Angela, his whole body was searching for answers, quick answers.

"First of all, stay calm. Breathe Joe. We can use this to our advantage, but, please, do not force it! Do not force anything! Let's see where the conversation takes us. I believe that with its natural flow, we'll be able to spot opportunities in order to help Maizey, and ultimately, to help everyone." She paused briefly, shaking her red hair, before she continued.

"Blue Bell is not here by chance. I firmly believe that she is *here* for a reason. So, let us use that reason to alleviate and ultimately resolve this whole upsetting setback." Angela loved using her hands while she spoke – she felt that one connected better this way and also, to get one's message across. And she had a lot of messages; hopefully they would be heard and begin to do their work, i.e. to bring about change.

"You always know what to say..."

"Now you're just making me blush. We all have answers inside of us. It is usually up to us to recognize them inside of us and then listen to them. Pay attention. That's all."

"Wow!"

"I hope tea is in order," Maizey almost sang her words as she danced her way to the coffee table balancing the enormous tray carefully. Blue Bell followed, Pup in one hand, and biscuits in the other.

Maizey instructed her where to sit – the grown-ups got to have their tea first. She silently obeyed, being still new at this game.

"Please, help yourselves," she invited Joe and Angela to some tea and also gestured towards the biscuits being displayed in a colourful bowl, "I made them this morning. Please, have some."

She sat patiently while waiting for them to finish. Once finished, she again ordered Blue Bell to have some biscuits. "No tea for you, young lady. You'll have to stick to milk for now." She watched Blue Bell like a hawk, making sure she only took a few biscuits *and* her sticky glass of milk.

She tried melting away into her deep seat, keeping Casey close.

Joe also watched her, but not like a hawk. He somehow felt responsible for her being here, in this volatile and messy situation. Poor girl, he thought and looked down at his warm cup of tea.

Angela was watching too. She was seeing potential everywhere. This could be quick and painless, but it all depended on Joe and Maizey. She dearly hoped that it would be quick and painless for both their sakes. This case has been dragging on for way too long. It needed a fix urgently, today still!

So, here goes...

"Maizey? May I please have another?" Blue Bell asked politely, being the first to break the continuous silence.

"Of course, dear," she answered right back. "But why are you calling me Maizey? I'm your Mama." She gave Blue Bell an intense stare, almost as if she was trying to strip away something.

"Eh," Blue Bell melted even further into her warm seat, holding Casey up as a potential shield.

"Maizey," Angela interrupted delicately, yet smoothly. "What tea is this? It goes well with these biscuits."

Maizey's focus was temporarily disrupted, but it was all that the redhead needed. She stood up and walked over to one of her display cases.

Maizey being Maizey, soon followed. She was very protective of her precious ornaments. "Please, don't touch them!" she instructed the slender redhead. She immediately pulled back her pale hand and rested them behind her back.

"Where did you get the green one? It looks so seventies..."

Her plan worked. Maizey was talking loudly, enthusiastically about her pride and joy. Her fleshy arms were all over the place, pointing this way, and that way.

Blue Bell smiled with instant relief as Angela winked at her and carried on with her line of questioning. If you looked at Angela point blank, you wouldn't say that this elegant, fashionably dressed, redhead was able to do what she did – disarming this conflict-filled and explosive situation.

Maizey turned around unexpectedly, apparently she was waiting for a response from absent-minded Joe. Her face turned into surprise as she asked, "What on God's green earth happened to your hair? Why is it blue?" Her arms were up in the air amplifying her surprise. "What the devil is going on here?"

Blue Bell was shifting uncomfortably about on her deep seat. Things were getting hot now, too hot for her. Given only half a chance, she would bounce. It didn't matter where to, as long as it was away from this mad house and these mad people.

Having seen the pure alarm on her delicate face, Joe suddenly stood up. All of a sudden, he looked like a giant, a Goliath who has risen from his slumber. Maizey took a step back, her full colourless lips shut tightly. She watched him like a hawk; he seemed bigger, more intimidating. She took another step back until she felt the glass display case behind her. She could hear her priceless ornaments rattling lightly behind her.

Angela wasn't fazed, not one bit. She stood fast; this was exactly what she wanted, it was exactly what she was waiting for... and finally, it happened – Joe stood up!

He came back to life!

Her light blue eyes were gleaming – this was therapy at its best!

"Maizey," Joe was now standing between a frightened teen and a woman who was beginning to see the light. Not a nice light, but light, at least!

"Ye, ye, yes Joe?" Maizey's lower lip was quivering slightly, her greyish eyes looked like two pools frozen in time.

"Maizey, it is all right." Joe took a step forward, slowly and in the softest voice he repeated his earnest words: "Maizey. Darling. It's all right."

Maizey just stared at him. It felt as if someone had sucked the very air out of her lungs. It felt as though her whole world was collapsing all around her. Like everything was coming to an end, a very, very fast end. Even her...

The very next moment, she fell to her knees and with her chubby hands in front of her face, she began to cry, sob. Her whole body was shaking violently with each sob. It pulled and tugged at her whole ageing frame.

Joe wanted to rush closer and comfort her, but Angela, the therapist, waived him off and formed with her red lips: give her a moment.

It was agonizing to watch, even for Blue Bell. Although she hasn't known Maizey that long, it was still hard to watch. Seeing and hearing so much pain, so much agony, so much sadness. She could even feel it, it had filled the entire room!

Angela nodded her OK to Joe; it was time now, time for them, these two people, to heal. Heal as best they could, as fast they could. At least then, they would have a chance at a happy, normal life. One they could both enjoy, for the rest of their lives (however long that may be...)

After a few more intense moments, Joe and Maizey stood hugging each other – something Blue Bell did not think she would ever see, and yet... here they were in a loving embrace. Almost as if the preceding twenty years, did not happen... did not exist...

Angela stood, arms folded lightly, smiling confidently, very pleased, looking real chuffed with herself. Another case closed, successfully.

Some time later...

It was a hot summer's day, *not* like any other. It was better.

Joe and Maizey sat peacefully on their familiar porch. They were drinking iced tea, sweetly flavoured with honey. Both were watching, their eyes filled with laughter, as Blue Bell, the blue-haired tamed 'teen', played with Casey on the front lawn.

Pup was not so pup anymore. He looked more and more like a real Jack Russell each day, and as always, cute as a button with his red-and-white bandanna.

Blue Bell filled the whole front yard with her laughter, touching every magnificent plant and every beautiful flower with it. She was having so much fun – playing with Casey in this magic-filled garden, being part of a whole and unbroken family.

It was like a dream come true!

"Blue, Blue, come have some tea," Joe called playfully. He liked having Blue Bell, 'Blue-girl', here. She was like a breath of fresh air. And the effect she had on Maizey – it was astounding!

"Here you go," Maizey said happily as she poured a glass for Blue Bell.

This child may have blue hair and be a bit eccentric at times, but she was more like a blue-haired angel to her, and she was lucky to have her in her life, in their lives!

"Lickedy-pickedy-lickedy-poop. Who is that?" They all looked up like one man at the female stranger climbing out of the yellow taxi cab.

A sudden, thick silence rained down on them; their light, fun laughter forgotten for the moment.

It was none other than Blue Bell's mom.

She (her mother) climbed out of the sunny cab with only one goal in mind: she had already lost one child, she did not want to lose another. She was here to make peace, not war, *and* to get her child back, her one and only child, Blue Bell.

Blue Bell was startled a bit at the sudden sight of her own mother. *But* she wasn't afraid.

This time, she wasn't alone. *She* had backing – the best kind – in the form of Joe, trucker Joe, and his lovely wife, Maizey...

The End

ABOUT THE AUTHOR

Jorgi initially studied psychology, but ended up writing instead. Thus she has followed her calling despite what the world dictated and have now finished her fourth book.